Charles Stanger Jerram

Graece Reddenda

Miscellaneous exercises for practice in Greek prose composition

Charles Stanger Jerram

Graece Reddenda
Miscellaneous exercises for practice in Greek prose composition

ISBN/EAN: 9783337368043

Printed in Europe, USA, Canada, Australia, Japan

Cover: Foto ©Andreas Hilbeck / pixelio.de

More available books at **www.hansebooks.com**

Clarendon Press Series

GRAECE REDDENDA

OR

MISCELLANEOUS EXERCISES

FOR PRACTICE IN

GREEK PROSE COMPOSITION

ARRANGED BY

C. S. JERRAM, M.A.

Late Scholar of Trinity College, Oxford
Editor of 'Luciani Vera Historia,' 'Cebetis Tabula,' 'Euripidis Alcestis,'
'Euripidis Helena,' 'Iphigenia in Tauris,' &c.

Oxford

AT THE CLARENDON PRESS

1889

PREFACE.

——◆——

This collection is a reprint, much enlarged and entirely re-arranged, from a previously published work bearing the same title. It is composed very much upon the same lines as my *Latine Reddenda*[1], which has been now for some time in use; and being intended solely for *practice*, not for instruction, it does not aim at competing with any existing manuals of Greek Prose Composition. The sentences in the first two Parts are designedly *miscellaneous*, and have been framed to illustrate all the most important constructions, without rules or references: they may be done on paper or *viva voce*, and either with or without previous preparation on the part of the pupil.

The First Part consists of exercises on the Simple Sentence and the Accidence of Grammar, and the first ten sections may be rendered nearly word for word into Greek by aid of the footnotes appended. The Second Part is on the Compound Sentence, and here, as well as in the later exercises of Part I, idiomatic phrases are introduced. The Third Part is designed as an introduction to continuous Greek Prose. The easier extracts, placed at the beginning of the part, may be tried, by way of variation, alternatively with the later sections of Parts I and II.

[1] *Latine Reddenda*, or Miscellaneous Sentences for Translation into Latin Prose. 6th Edition. 1888. Longmans & Co.

By words and phrases in *italics* attention is drawn to
differences of idiom, but such suggestions are more sparingly
supplied in the later sentences and extracts, and are alto-
gether dispensed with in the last ten or twelve pieces of
the Third Part.

A Vocabulary was felt to be necessary, as few boys are
provided with an English-Greek Lexicon; but only such
words are given (besides nouns and verbs) as are not easily
accessible from the grammar, and care has been taken to
supply as little information as possible upon idiomatic phrases
or syntax constructions. For passages in which much
turning and recasting of the sentence is needed, a vocabulary
for the most part merely verbal cannot of course be of much
use; but where a more or less literal rendering will serve,
the present Vocabulary will, it is hoped, be found sufficient
for the purpose.

In the notice prefixed to the Appendix I have referred the
student to Mr. Sidgwick's Notes on Idioms and Metaphors.
His observations on the Abstract and Concrete (§§ 97–106),
with the corresponding examples, deserve, I think, special
attention. It is of course the fact that both forms of expression occur in Thucydides and other classical authors,
often in close connexion with each other. A good instance
may be quoted from Thuc. iii. 82, in his account of the
troubles at Corcyra :—

(1) τόλμα μὲν ἀλόγιστος ἀνδρία ἐνομίσθη, μέλλησις δὲ προμηθὴς
δειλία εὐπρεπής. '*Reckless daring was regarded as courage,
prudent hesitation as specious cowardice.*'

(2) ὁ μὲν χαλεπαίνων πιστὸς ἀεί, ὁ δὲ ἀντιλέγων αὐτῷ ὕποπτος.

'*He who advocated cruel measures was always trusted, while his opponent was suspected.*' Or in abstract form:—'*Advocacy of cruel measures always inspired confidence, while the opposite course was made a ground of suspicion.*'

But it is no less true that the Greek *natural* mode of expression preferred the concrete to the abstract form, as in the second example from Thucydides, and it is in this form that the abstract sentences in the Appendix should be recast before translating them.

Of personal and place-names only such are inserted in the Vocabulary as differ, however slightly, from the Latin or English forms (as *Corcyra,* Κέρκυρα, *Athens,* Ἀθῆναι, &c.). Those in which transliteration follows a recognised rule (as *Cyrus,* Κῦρος, *Boeotia,* Βοιωτία, &c.) are purposely omitted. The vowels *e* and *o*, if *long*, are so marked in the text, except final -*es* ; otherwise they are understood to be *short.*

CHARLES S. JERRAM.

OXFORD, *January*, 1889.

PRELIMINARY EXERCISES

PREPOSITIONS.

———•———

Translate into Greek —

Up the river — through the land — during the war — from Greece into Asia — along with Dēmosthenes — according to law — throughout Greece — all night long — above the sky (οὐρανός) — down the hill (λόφος) — for this purpose — instead of me — by my means — after this — at Marathon — in preference to this — out of Italy — towards Samos — about sunset (ἡλίου δυσμαί) — near the river — on your account — contrary to law — towards evening — wherefore ? — therefore — under ground — on this occasion — on these conditions — on horseback — at this time — up to my time — as far as the town — for the sake of money — next to me — upon the earth — besides all this — in presence of the judges — in consequence of this — homewards — against the king — the way to happiness (εὐδαιμονία).

Beyond hope — throughout my life (βίος) — at daybreak — in addition to this — in return for a favour (χάρις) — from Cyrus to the king — by my side — with a view to justice (δικαιοσύνη) — among men — in the reign of Darius — made of gold — in front of the gates — in the meantime — in (the house) of Callias — by fifties — at intervals of five — year after year — in behalf of Sōcrates — in company with the women — to the number of twenty — born before me — born of noble (εὐγενής) parents — every ninth year — according to my wishes — beyond the

Hellēspont — day by day — side by side — in sight of gods and men — piety (εὐσέβεια) towards the gods — at a distance of ten stades — in defence of his country — descended from Hēra-cles — one by one — over a hundred men — about noon (μεσημβρία) — in the days of our fathers — in my judgment — in earnest — of his own accord — unexpectedly — of a truth — in-doors — house by house — justly.

With many tears (δάκρυ) — on both sides of the town — at nightfall — four deep — to get wisdom (σοφία) — contrary to reason (λόγος) — on board a ship — by the gods' help — little by little — on all occasions — twenty to one — seasonably — with all his might (κράτος) — on the Athenians' side — under arms — blood-relations — ever since the war — a hundred-fold — to a large extent — with an eye to advantage (κέρδος) — in proportion — to my advantage — owing to circumstances — on the present occasion — for what purpose? — as far as in you lies — subject to Darius — from his youth up — from hear-say — at a given signal (σημεῖον) — henceforth — on his oath (ὅρκος) — to the music of the flute (αὐλός) — by word of mouth — with all my heart — the disciples of Plato — as far as I am concerned — as far as is necessary (δεῖ) — our own rela-tions — the history of Greece — with a view to my injury — (descended) on the mother's side.

This depends on you — this was done by Cratippus — I did it all by myself — they marched in single file — they fight for their safety — he came at nightfall — he spoke at length — they fought on our side — he is weak (ἀσθενής) in proportion to his size (μέγεθος) — you came in season — I will try (πειρῶμαι) to the extent of my power — the ships sailed in column — he is wise compared with Callistratus — I value (ποιοῦμαι) this highly — he was in a state of fear — I knew Socrates by sight — this is the way along the river — he fell upon the ground — he is seated (κάθημαι) on a tree — the cave (σπέος n.) is under the rock (πέτρα) — he went to Athens to Sōphrŏniscus — they rush (φέρομαι) upon the foe — he came up to the wall — let us sail for Greece — they are going on guard (φυλακή) — Clearchus was posted (τάσσω) on the right (wing) — you did it in anger — he is (engaged) in business (πράγματα) — I asked (καλέω) him to dinner (δεῖπνον) — this I received (δέχομαι) from my father — this happened at the close of the war — after (being) rich he became poor — but for Xenophon this would not have happened (*aor. ind. with* ἄν).

Translate into English —

Ἐκ δεξιᾶς — διὰ πολλοῦ — ἀνὰ τὴν πόλιν — ἀπὸ σημείου — ἐν τούτῳ — ἐν δίκῃ — ἀνθ᾽ ὧν — σὺν τῷ χρόνῳ — ἀπὸ δείπνου — ἐξ ἴσου — δι᾽ ἡμέρας — δι᾽ ἡμῶν — δι᾽ ἡμᾶς — κατὰ τῆς πέτρας — ἀφ᾽ οὗ — ἐκ τῶν νόμων — ἐκ τούτου — ἐκ τούτων — ἐν Ἅιδου — σὺν τῷ νόμῳ — δι᾽ ὀλίγου — εἰς δύναμιν — ἀντὶ τούτων — ἐκ χαλκοῦ — μετὰ ταῦτα — μετὰ τούτων — ἐφ᾽ ἵππου — παρὰ δύναμιν — ἐπὶ τούτοις — ἐπὶ τὸ πολύ — μεθ᾽ ἡμέραν — ὑπὲρ ἐλπίδα — παρὰ ταῦτα — παρὰ τὸν νόμον — κατὰ μικρὸν — κατὰ τί; — κατὰ ῥόον — ἐπὶ νεώς — ἐπὶ τῷ παρόντι — πρὸς θεῶν — πρὸς τούτοις — πρὸς ταῦτα — ὑπὸ νύκτα — διὰ ταῦτα — ἀνὰ κράτος — ἀπὸ τοῦδε — ἐκ τῶν παρόντων — ἐν ᾧ — διὰ τρίτου ἔτους — διὰ τί; — κατὰ τοῦ ὕδατος — ἐπὶ τοῖς πράγμασι — τὸ ἐφ᾽ ἡμῖν — ἐφ᾽ ὅρκου — παρὰ δόξαν — παρ᾽ ἡμέραν — διὰ τάχους — κατὰ τάχος — ὑπὲρ ἑκατόν — ὑπὲρ τῆς πατρίδος — καθ᾽ ἡμέραν — κατὰ θάλασσαν — ἐπὶ δύο ἡμέρας — παρ᾽ ὀλίγον — πρὸς τῷ ἄρχοντι — πρὸς καιρόν — ὑφ᾽ ἑαυτῷ — ὑφ᾽ ἑαυτοῦ — τὰ ἀμφὶ τὸν πόλεμον.

Ἀνὰ πέντε ὀβολούς — οἱ ἐκ τῆς πόλεως — ἀπὸ καιροῦ — οἱ ἀπὸ σκηνῆς — ἐκ τοῦ φανεροῦ — ἐμοῦ γε ἕνεκα — οἱ ἐν τέλει — οἱ σὺν Κλεάρχῳ — δι᾽ ἄγνοιαν — ἐπ᾽ ἐμοῦ — ἐπ᾽ ἐμοί — παρὰ πάντα τὸν βίον — ἀμφὶ ἀγορὰν πλήθουσαν — οἱ μετὰ Σωκράτους — κατὰ φύσιν — οἱ καθ᾽ ἡμᾶς — κατ᾽ ἄνδρα — τὰ ἐπὶ Θρᾳκῆς — ὁ ἐπὶ τῶν ἱππέων — πρὸς τὰ παρόντα — πρὸς ἡδονὴν λέγειν — ὑπὸ σάλπιγγος πορεύεσθαι — αὐτὸς πρὸς ἑαυτὸν — οὐ πρὸς σοῦ ἐστι — τὰ πρὸς τοὺς

θεούς — ὑπὸ Κύρου ἐπράχθη — ἐπὶ κέρως πλεῖν — τὰ κατὰ τὴν
πόλιν — κατὰ γνώμην λέγειν — ἐπὶ Κύρου βασιλεύοντος — οἱ περὶ
Πυθαγόραν — τὸ ἐπὶ τοῦτον εἶναι — ἐφ' ὅσον δεῖ — παρ' οὐδὲν
ποιεῖσθαι — περὶ πολλοῦ ποιεῖσθαι — ἐπὶ πέντε τάσσεσθαι — ὑπὲρ
ἐμέ ἐστιν — κατὰ πόλεις οἰκεῖσθαι — καθ' ἡσυχίαν ζῆν — παρὰ
Καλλίαν εἰσιέναι — εἰς τετάρτην ἐλθεῖν — εἰς τὴν στρατιὰν λέγειν —
ἐκ χειρὸς μάχεσθαι — διὰ δέκα ἐτῶν — διὰ χειρός ἔχειν — διὰ λόγων
ἰέναι — κατά τινος λέγειν — ἀπὸ κλοπῆς ζῆν — ναῦς ἐς πεντήκοντα —
εἰς τέσσαρας πορεύεσθαι — διὰ μακρῶν λέγειν — ἐν αἰτίᾳ ἔχειν —
ἐπὶ Σικελίας πλεῖν — εἰς πᾶν ἀφῖκται — μείζων ἢ κατ' ἄνθρωπον —
παρὰ μικρὸν ἐλθεῖν κινδύνου.

GRAECE REDDENDA.

FIRST PART.

I.

1. The soldiers are fighting bravely.
2. The Athenians fought (*imperf.*) seven days (*acc.*).
3. A certain man had thirteen sons.
4. This woman shall have a fine hen.
5. This man is my brother's friend.
6. I admired (*aor.*) the beauty of your horse.
7. The judge often admired (*imperf.*) the orators.
8. The little boy became a great man.
9. The old man's son will guide us on (ἐν) the way.
10. Cyrus will march against (ἐπὶ *with acc.*) the king of the Assyrians.
11. All the soldiers have now (ἤδη) returned home.
12. I will give you (some) cold water.
13. The boy was-pursuing the hare.
14. The Athenians will elect Lamachus general.
15. The carpenter has made a wooden table.
16. The Greeks worshipped (*imperf.*) many gods.

II.

17. There-were many dogs in my house.
18. The sons of the Persians learnt (*imperf.*) truth and justice.

B

19. I built (*aor.*) yonder tall[1] white tower.
20. It is pleasant to drink good wine.
21. The young birds will soon have (φύω) feathers.
22. The army was not able to advance further.
23. The citizens opened the gates of the town.
24. All the country was ravaged by (ὑπὸ *with gen.*) the Greeks.
25. Every town was captured and burnt.
26. It is hard to deceive the wise and prudent (men).
27. The boy has deceived the master himself.
28. The same master will punish the boy.
29. You will not drink-up all this water.
30. This young-man is taller than his[2] father.
31. The girl dances better (*adv.*) than her[2] mother.
32. Fortune always helps brave men.

III.

33. Many fishes are-in the great[3] wide sea.
34. The animal, which you saw yesterday, is called an elephant.
35. The good son honours his[4] father and his[4] mother.
36. Nobody wishes to be thought (δοκεῖν) foolish.
37. Nature has given us two ears[5] and one tongue.
38. Stand here; give me your[4] hand.
39. Twenty-seven ships were taken in this great war.
40. I will show you all the spoil which I have taken.
41. Who says that the boy is not very wise?
42. Cyrus entered Babylōnia with all his[4] army.
43. A certain woman had four large dogs.
44. We found five eggs in the nest yesterday.

---

[1] Say 'tall *and* white.'
[2] Use the article for the possessive pronoun.
[3] See note 1.   [4] See note 2.   [5] Use μὲν .... δέ.

45. The dog carried a bone in his[1] mouth to his[1] master.

46. A (τις) man, meeting (*aor.*) a boar in the forest, ran-away.

47. A large tree has fallen-down in the garden.

48. Cyrus often hunted wild-beasts in his[1] park.

IV.

49. Darius married Atossa, the daughter of Cyrus.

50. After twenty-seven years the boy became a judge.

51. It does not become a modest man to praise himself.

52. What I have promised to-day I will perform to-morrow.

53. I knew an old man, Charicles by-name (*acc.*).

54. He threw a black stone over the wall into the town.

55. Cyrus sent-for Orontes, a Persian captain, into his[1] tent.

56. The captive, having burst (*aor.*) his[1] bonds, is now free.

57. Women always admire men who (ὅστις) are brave and handsome.

58. A (τις) soldier slew Cyrus with a javelin (when) fighting against (πρὸς) his[1] brother.

59. Eurybates asked his[1] friend (for) fifteen talents.

60. I have asked you this (question) four times already.

61. The judges did not decide that matter rightly.

62. The rivers of Italy are larger than the rivers of Greece.

63. The cat catches no[2] fish for-fear (*dat.*) of the water.

64. Not all the Athenians understood the wisdom of Sōcrates.

V.

65. A large[3] black dog has bitten my[4] right foot.

66. You have eaten the three apples which I put in the dining-room.

---

[1] See note 2, p. 2.   [2] Say 'does *not* catch.'
[3] See note 1, p. 2.   [4] Express the pronoun here.

67. Sōsthenes was the slave of a most cruel master.

68. It is not easy to forget an injury.

69. I never knew a better man than Philōn.

70. .The ambassador went-away by night (*gen.*) alone.

71. I did not think that you were so foolish.

72. Veni, vidi, vici.

73. He hurled his enemy from the rock into the sea.

74. Arise, brave men, and follow me to the battle !

75. The sharpest axe cannot cut iron.

76. The chariots were borne through the midst of the enemy's (*pl.*) army.

77. Gold and silver and copper were found in this district.

78. This is certainly a most clever child.

79. The disciples of Pythagoras, the Samian, would (ἐθέλω) not eat beans.

80. Multas urbes cepit, multos homines occīdit.

VI.

81. A[1] brave soldier will not surrender his arms to the enemy.

82. Three wise judges dwell-in this city.

83. Naxos was taken by the Persians.

84. The citizens brought corn wine and oil in vessels.

85. A great work has been done in Greece to-day.

86. The gods are propitious to the good and brave.

87. In winter we use two or even three blankets, in summer one only.

88. The Greek army marched against the Persian king.

89. Chilōn's wife's brother has been crowned in the market-place.

90. The Persians will ravage all the Scythian land.

[1] Definite article.

91. Cyrus, riding from the battle, laughs-at *his*[1] *pursuers.*

92. I will not deceive my good father and my dear mother.

93. The finest gold shall be given to Philip himself.

94. I saw the same man yesterday and to-day.

95. The army (στρατός) of the Persians have I often seen marching in order.

96. The unjust master has flogged his faithful slave.

VII.

97. We all love ourselves more than we love others.

98. Dulce est forti viro pro patria mori.

99. They persuaded me to set-up a strong wall round my garden.

100. We will not teach our children to do wrong.

101. Lycurgus enacted severe laws for the Lacedaemonians.

102. Those thieves have stolen the money out of my strong chest.

103. There-are three pigeons on the roof of yonder house.

104. The wise poet read the king's letter in silence.

105. The Indian is-asleep under the high tree's shade.

106. Cyrus did not fear to accept the omen.

107. The boy was pleased (at) seeing his companion punished.

108. The ships of the Greeks anchored in the harbour of Calpē.

109. The father gave his son a bag full of gold.

---

[1] Say 'those pursuing.'

110. The boy standing [1] on the bank will soon bathe in the river.

111. Darius (when) about to die sent-for his two sons.

112. Athenienses Solōnem summo honore habebant.

VIII.

113. The son of Callias was lame (in) both his feet (*acc.*).

114. A tree falling-on (*aor.*) the slave's leg, broke the bone.

115. 'You will die in this town,' said the prophet to Alexander.

116. Thus Agias avenged-himself-upon all his enemies.

117. Having said many such [2] (words) he departed homewards.

118. At home we employ both men and women (as) slaves.

119. The farmer found a hare hidden in his house.

120. He has cut-off the boy's finger with a sharp knife.

121. I saw seventy-five sheep and forty-two oxen in yonder field.

122. Having drawn his sword he cut-off his neighbour's ear.

123. This teacher will not spare the ignorant boy.

124. Ingratum me esse nemo unquam dicet.

125. Alcibiades received the envoys in the town-hall.

126. Lamachus and Nicias were both skilled in the art of war.

127. Some boys are lazy, others work willingly.

128. The town [3] (of) Sparta is not very large.

---

[1] Express the article before 'standing.'

[2] Neuter plural.

[3] Reverse the order of nouns.

IX.

129. We have left our wives and children at (ἐν) Athens.

130. From Sardis to Babylōn is a long journey.

131. I have never seen the island [1] (of) Cyprus.

132. Who has killed the chickens in my garden?

133. O fair Calypsō, do not (μὴ) trust Odysseus.

134. All the towns of the Scythians have been destroyed by (ὑπὸ) the enemy.

135. Eo praelio milites ducenti et triginta perierunt.

136. Use not many words before the king.

137. Lend Hippias the three talents which I gave you.

138. Return me the money which you borrowed.

139. My father returned to-day from Athens.

140. What I promise to-day I will give you to-morrow.

141. Instead of a loaf the woman has found a stone.

142. Come hither, little-boy, and learn wisdom.

143. Fortune always helps brave men.

144. Cyrus was killed in battle by a Carian soldier.

X.

145. A stronger man than Xenocleides who can find?

146. Artembares died at Babylōn by his own hand.

147. The horn of the rhinoceros is very strong and thick.

148. Walking along the road a philosopher fell into a well.

149. I cannot persuade this boy to obey his master.

150. Facilius est ducere exercitum quam vincere hostes.

151. Juno was said to be both sister and wife of Jupiter.

152. The carpenter brought-in the table which I ordered him to make.

153. But I could not use the table which the carpenter had-brought (*aor.*).

[1] See note 3, p. 6.

154. He gave Philōn four talents, Callias nothing.

155. Who does not know that twenty is twice ten?

156. But a (τις) boy once said that twice eleven was twenty-one.

157. Clearchus fled with his army into the town.

158. The others[1] had left the city, but you remained there.

159. I cannot give you the money which I promised you.

160. This is not the road which leads to Athens.

161. My wife, the goose and I[2] dined together.

162. After dinner we could not find the goose.

XI.

163. I saw not only Callicles, but his wife and son also.

164. Be thou crowned (*perf. pass.*), blest city, with the fairest rewards of virtue.

165. Nobody ever heard such a thing from *anyone*.

166. The *fact that* all men are mortal is known to all.

167. Having heard this, Darius made war against the Scythians.

168. Some[1] praise Eumenes for this, others blame him.

169. You are always telling the same story.

170. The eagle *flew-down and* seated itself on the plough.

171. Eleven dogs had only fifteen ears.

172. The barbarians were conquered at the battle of (ἐν) Marathōn.

173. The lamb fled-for-refuge into a temple.

174. He escaped the wolf[1], but was sacrificed by the priest.

175. I will not put on my red cloak to-day.

176. Do not conceal this fault from your father.

177. He put a garland of white roses on the girl's head.

178. I have often envied you your good-fortune.

[1] Use μὲν ... δέ.   [2] Put ἐγὼ first.

XII.

179. You will surely miss your way in the dark.

180. Thrasybūlus was accused of many strange crimes.

181. It is *the duty of* children to honour and love their parents.

182. The dog caught-hold-of the wolf by the right ear.

183. I have not met your brother for two days.

184. We must try to persuade the girl to obey her mother.

185. Would that Sōcrates were now alive!

186. *I wish* I had been with you and Critōn yesterday.

187. I will give you *some of* the apples which I have bought.

188. Stop talking and laughing, boys, directly!

189. You have not managed the affairs of the state well.

190. For fifteen stades we were marching through a desert country.

191. The *son of* Philip will command the army for many days.

192. *He who does not love* his father and mother is impious.

193. The Greeks have sailed across the sea in sixty-seven ships.

194. Cyrus sets out with fifteen horsemen for Sardis.

XIII.

195. The archers shot each his own arrow.

196. I cannot use all the books which I have.

197. Of all men I know you are the most temperate.

198. Dēmosthenes happened *to-be-present* at that meeting.

199. Callippus is said to have swum across the river.

200. *He who has* an ungrateful child is miserable.

201. My brother *had-a-pain in* both his ears.

202. A good citizen must (δεῖ) obey the rulers of the city.

203. Quis autem Sōcrate sapientior esse poterat?

204. He told me to come to him after dinner.

205. I told him that this would be impossible.

206. Solōn was grieved *at* (ἐπὶ) *the citizens being poor*.

207. *Those who love* virtue shall manage all my affairs.

208. The *son of* Philip loves my brother's daughter.

209. I will go at once to the king and ask him for money.

210. Xerxes beheld *with astonishment*[1] the *destruction of*[1] his whole army.

XIV.

211. *Riding* is pleasant and-not (οὐδὲ) very hard to learn.

212. *By trying* to do a few things well you will soon learn much (*pl.*).

213. These four thieves have stript my brother of his clothes.

214. Those whom we thought to be men were said to be women.

215. Animals feed on grass, men eat the animals themselves.

216. It is not in your power to become a philosopher.

217. The elephant is superior in size to the camel.

218. Great was the joy *with which* we welcomed the conqueror.

219. The wife of Callistratus was *evidently* mad.

220. I will tell you all I know about the affair.

221. Do not accuse the man of so-great a crime.

222. The boy *who is* in the water will soon swim.

223. Themistocles Athenis *expulsus* in Epīrum vēnit.

224. This boy stood on the wall (and) then jumped down.

225. The barbarians turned and fled *as fast as possible*.

226. Is there anyone on the earth stronger than Milo?

---

[1] Express by participles of the corresponding verbs.

XV.

227. Who bade you go with your brother into the town?

228. Was not Actaeōn devoured by his own dogs?

229. It is impossible for one body to have three heads.

230. He snatched up my wife's cloak with both his hands.

231. The tower stands on the top of the hill of Myrae.

232. None of the horses which I have shall be given to Critias.

233. You are not at all worthy of so great an honour.

234. He is said to have surrounded the city with a wall *of brass.*

235. They returned to the place whence they had started the day before.

236. Here we saw twelve ships sailing along the coast towards Sinōpē.

237. Cyrus was at that time marching away-from the river Tigris.

238. This man was a friend whom Callippus trusted greatly.

239. 'It is better,' said he, 'to die than to live in the midst of enemies.'

240. I have not met either my own friend or my brother's.

241. Many men desire to have *what belongs to* their neighbours.

242. Why do you not try to do what I bid you?

XVI.

243. Who said, 'one swallow does not make a spring'?

244. The Greek cavalry charging the Persian ranks routed them.

245. All good citizens *should* defend the laws of their country.

246. Once thirty tyrants ruled the city of Athens.

247. You touched me once, but you shall not touch me twice.

248. A good soldier must obey his captain.

249. Antiphōn, the captain, treats his sailors well.

250. Quos nunquam vidimus, eos saepe diligimus.

251. Drink (2 *aor.*) this wine, Hippocrates, which I have given you.

252. Taking a sharp axe in his hand he cut down the tree.

253. Do we not seem to you to be acting foolishly?

254. Go ye home, boys, (and) rest from your labours.

255. He was a friend to most (men), an enemy to no one.

256. *Victis hostibus* exercitum in castra reduxit.

257. Most young men love riding.

258. I saw him riding in the street to-day.

XVII.

259. He broke his neck by falling from his horse.

260. The king of *Persia* has by some been called a barbarian.

261. Plato taught his disciples much strange philosophy.

262. The dog has bitten the girl with his sharp teeth.

263. Hares have short legs and long ears.

264. Charmides, *quum haec vidisset*, magnopere miratus est.

265. *By-help-of* the gods we have conquered the king's armies.

266. It is disgraceful not to do good to one's friends.

267. Both you and I have often been deceived by Agathōn.

268. The allies ran-away *for-fear-of* the enemy.

269. I left him standing in the middle of the road.

270. Callias, admodum juvenis, Megaclis filiam duxit.

271. Neither women nor children were found in this city.

272. The man is not brave, nor is he prudent.

273. Meanwhile Clearchus came up with all his forces.

274. He was struck by a stone while-walking in the street.

XVIII.

275. The child by shouting disturbed his mother greatly.

276. We are accustomed to love those who do good to us.

277. The whole country was being ravaged, but Brasidas saved it.

278. He has just come from the province of which he is satrap.

279. Some men told me one (story), some another.

280. Having placed his stick on the table, he *sat down and wrote a letter.*

281. After-ascending the mountain we surveyed the whole district.

282. *Mortuum esse* Cyrum Graecorum nesciebant legati.

283. Thus saying he departed to his own city.

284. I perceived *that you were* not a very wise man.

285. *Forte erat* quidam Athenis senex, nomine Philocleōn.

286. Beyond the river was a wall twenty feet high.

287. Phalinus, sent by the king, bade the Greeks surrender their arms.

288. A nightingale, sitting on a high oak, was singing sweetly.

289. I do not suppose that the town has been taken to-day.

290. *On-the-death-of* Cyrus, Cambyses became king of Persia.

XIX.

291. Diōn having driven Dionysius from his kingdom, heard that Callippus was plotting against him.

292. The city of Syracuse was besieged by the Athenians for many days.

293. The fox looking up into the tree bade the cock come down.

294. Lamachus shouting to Hēgēsippus told him to wait for him.

295. *But* he would not stop, *but* rode on at full speed.

296. This he did *without the knowledge* of the general.

297. Upon hearing this Darius made war upon the Scythians.

298. You must not do this, but you may do that.

299. Dēmosthenis filia *aspectu* pulcherrima est.

300. I *arrived before* you at Ephesus.

301. *At my request* the envoys came to dinner.

302. He stopped me *in the middle of my speech.*

303. Will you not help my brother who has lately become poor?

304. The foe *that submits* we ought to spare.

305. What you say is nothing else than folly.

306. What all men desire few are worthy to obtain.

XX.

307. 'Do you,' said he, 'know Alcibiades *by sight?*'

308. You are not even a wise man, much less a philosopher.

309. *As far as I know,* what you say is true.

310. He says that he himself is master here.

311. This was done *on my account* but not *by my means.*

312. Not one of these things is *in my power* to accomplish.

313. Nemo est qui (ὅστις) tyrannum non oderit.

314. *The* more a man has, *the* more he often desires.

315. All this happened *during the reign* of Antiochus.

316. We must defend our country and take vengeance on her foes.

317. You have done a *wonderful amount* of work in a very short time.

318. I would gladly oblige *a man like* Charicles.

319. Ad summum montem ab hostibus prima luce perventum est.

320. I would not say such a thing *in my father's hearing*.

321. The oftener I meet Cleisthenes the more I dislike him.

322. Did you restore the money to my brother, or not?

XXI.

323. Dionysius, banished from Syracuse, *kept a school* at Corinth.

324. It is an old saying that a fool knows not how to *hold his tongue*.

325. Agias threw himself into the sea and escaped to shore by swimming.

326. The right wing was commanded by Cyaxares, the left by Cyrus.

327. A just man not only does no wrong, but does not even desire to do so.

328. Barbari paulisper morati mox *abjectis armis* fugiunt.

329. An ape perched on a tree was watching the reapers *at their work*.

330. Stones thrown by Deucaliōn at the command of Zeus *were turned into* men.

331. Pyrrhus, rex Epīri, peritissimus belli fuisse dicitur.

332. The wealthier a man is, the more unhappy he often is.

333. Cleander went into exile *by his friends' advice*.

334. Seeing is believing, but it is often hard to see (things) clearly.

335. Will you give up the letter which you stole from me yesterday?

336. Is not a cloud sometimes very like a dolphin?

337. On hearing this we all went back to Naples at once.

338. Graeci eos, qui sua lingua non utebantur, barbaros appellabant.

XXII.

339. The Persians taught their children temperance and *obedience* to their elders.

340. *Silence* is better for a 'man than *vain and rash speaking*.

341. Whom the gods love die young.

342. Sōsthenes wept bitterly *at the news of* his son's death.

343. Some saved themselves by flight, the rest were taken and put to death.

344. Epicydes, having lost his right foot, made himself a wooden one.

345. He stood at the gate *with* a drawn sword in his hand.

346. It is not *every one who can* foresee the future.

347. This table, if sold, might perhaps fetch twenty-five obols.

348. It is the nature of children to pursue what is agreeable.

349. I wish you had acted more discreetly.

350. Here is the boy *who sings* well: I heard him singing yesterday.

351. He got up and went out *in the middle of his dinner*.

352. Do not envy your neighbours their possessions.

353. What ever am I to do with such a son as this?

354. He seems to have acted rashly rather than courageously.

XXIII.

355. All this happened *in the time of* Thēseus king of Athens.

356. There is *no difference between* a coward and a slave.

357. The village is distant about four miles from Ephesus.

358. This boy has been hit on the head with a sharp stone.

359. The land was said to flow with milk and honey.

360. Fur puerum domum redeuntem vestibus spoliavit.

361. Callias sold his horse for as much as he *gave for it.*

362. He who is contented with a little is richer than Croesus himself.

363. The man fled away by night, leaving his wife behind him.

364. Thereupon the soldiers sat down and refused to proceed further.

365. Meanwhile Lysias held his tongue, but Philēsias got up and spoke as follows.

366. Next day we reached a large town on the sea-coast, named Myriandus.

367. The wall was built sixteen feet in width and forty-seven in height.

368. Some people think gold is less valuable than iron.

369. The boy seems to have forgotten all that his master taught him.

370. He says the house he is building will soon be finished.

XXIV.

371. Utrum canis lupo est similior an vulpi?

372. I did not deem him worthy of so great honour.

373. Listen to me, boys, who am now teaching you philosophy.

c

374. I have now nearly as much money as I want.

375. There is *no trusting* a traitor's promise.

376. When only *nine years old* Hannibal swore he would be an enemy to the Romans.

377. You returned yesterday, but did not return the book I lent you.

378. Quod nobis aufert, id amicis donat.

379 This boy spends most of his time in doing nothing.

380. Why have you not repented of your faults?

381. God moves the world; the earth moves round the sun.

382. It is the duty of a good sovereign to guard his people well.

383. Methinks the opinion of Sōcrates is better than that of Alcibiades.

384. No man was ever wiser than Socrates, but he himself said he was not wise.

385. Plato said that a good man will never fear death.

386. What I have *been about* is no concern of yours.

XXV.

387. Cleitus was slain by Alexander when drunk at a banquet.

388. We saw 8,400 hoplites, 12,780 peltasts, and 1140 ships.

389. Sua cuique reddere aliquando difficillimum est.

390. *After the capture of* the town the general put all the citizens to death.

391. Charicles has been condemned to death *in his absence*.

392. How many of us when old remember what we learnt as boys?

393. Whatever I could find in the house *I brought away with me.*

394. You seem to be very *easily persuaded* to do wrong.

395. Callias is five years younger than his brother Euthyphron.

396. Am I not that Miltiades, who defeated the Persians at Marathōn?

397. *A man like* Sōsthenes is loved and respected by all.

398. In the tomb a body was found *of superhuman size.*

399. Most women love the adornment of the body; many adorn their minds also.

400. Sōphroniscus is not thought to have acted unjustly in this matter.

401. It is the duty of a wise and prudent man to submit to necessity.

402. Nobody has ever said that you are either a handsome or a clever boy.

XXVI.

403. We waited several days for the approach of the enemy, who never made their appearance.

404. I entreat you by all the gods, depart hence immediately.

405. At daybreak we reached the top of the hill, whence the sea was *clearly visible.*

406. Whatever a man gets *by unfair means* is *no true* gain to him.

407. Everything being now got ready, the soldiers issued from the camp armed for battle.

408. Why do you not tell the same story to-day that you told yesterday?

409. To act as you intend would be expedient rather than according to justice.

410. Lacedaemoniorum castra duobus milibus passuum a mari aberant.

411. News was brought to Cyrus that the Assyrians were riding up *at full gallop.*

412. Ancient Syracuse is said to have been the largest and the most beautiful of all the towns in Sicily.

413. Tell me, Callias, have you ever heard of people living in the moon ?

414. So he sent for the man at once, and bade him come to him on the following day.

415. Hearing this the general decided to proceed by land.

416. Nemo mortalium *omnibus horis* sapit.

417. It will be very difficult to cross the river just now *in the face of* a pursuing host.

418. Thereupon some of the soldiers raised a shout, others ran to the camp for help.

XXVII.

419. On perceiving the Greek cavalry the enemy fled faster than before.

420. Go away directly ! the *mere fact of* your being here annoys me much.

421. Boys *nowadays* seem to learn a great deal their fathers never knew.

422. But every sort of learning is not profitable, nor even harmless.

423. Not many days ago Agias was prosecuted for theft, but the judges acquitted him.

424. I should not like to take hold of a mad bull by his horns.

425. Unperceived by the guards at the gate the enemy entered the town by night.

426. This sorrow of mine is *too great for tears.*

427. Lysias was an orator who always spoke *at great length.*

428. Our common safety *depends on* you alone.

429. It is not *my wish* that you should remain in ignorance.

430. I should be glad to hear what Dēmosthenes will say in reply to this.

431. Once a man wishing to cross a river went into the boat on horseback.

432. Someone asking him the reason, he replied, 'I want to cross more quickly.'

433. A simpleton, wishing his horse not to eat too much, gave him no food.

434. When the horse died, he was astonished and said 'My horse had just learnt to live on nothing, and then he died.'

SECOND PART.

I.

1. No one knew what the king was about to do.
2. What Theobūlus said in the council pleased everybody.
3. He bought a horse whenever he came to Ephesus.
4. When I have seen Callicles I will tell you the cause of this.
5. If you have (any) money give some to the poor.
6. If I had known this before, I would not have punished him.
7. If I were to ask you, perhaps you would not be able to answer.
8. You ought not to be at a loss now what *to do*.
9. Many of the soldiers were not there *to receive* their pay.
10. The master is far *too* clever *to be* deceived by the boy.
11. He went *with ten others* to see the great king.
12. He will march with a large army to fight against the Persians.
13. If I teach my boy impudence, he will insult me.
14. I am come to Athens to see the works of Praxiteles.
15. By acting thus you will *clearly not learn* wisdom.
16. I clearly understood what you told me yesterday.

II.

17. Forgive me if I do not speak plainly.
18. No one, unless he were mad, would say such a thing.

19. I promised to be there on the fifteenth day of the ninth month.

20. At quid impedit *quominus* hoc facias?

21. I had nowhere *to go to*, and now I have nothing *to do*.

22. He said *that he* had killed the man himself.

23. He said that not *he himself*, but Nicias was commander.

24. I asked the old man what he was doing at home.

25. Who said that all virtue consisted in loving one's relations?

26. Sōcrates, si vere sapiens fuisset, vinum non ebibisset.

27. Postquam ad pontem advenerant, qui in *extremo agmine* erant constitere.

28. Will you not fight if the enemy appear to-day?

29. Tell me *where* you are going to-morrow.

30. Tell me where you were yesterday.

31. Wait for me here until I come to you.

32. You did not wait for me there until I came.

III.

33. He said that if I did this he would praise me.

34. I went away so as not to see the stranger.

35. I was away yesterday so that I did not see your father.

36. He came to see if the work was finished.

37. He asked me whether my father was at home.

38. There is no one here to do this great work.

39. He is *too* wise *to be* angry at this.

40. I deny *that I* have ever deceived you.

41. Who is so blind as not to see the sun?

42. There are some who do not know what virtue is.

43. Vereor *ut* prudens sis, Antipho.

44. Veritus sum *ne* in hac re errares.

45. Before the sun rose he appeared before the king.

46. As soon as I have seen your father I will come to you.

47. *There is no trusting* the son of Cleinias even *on his oath*.

48. *The fact of* my having been here yesterday does not concern you at all.

IV.

49. The doctor did not know what *was the matter with* the child.

50. I have been waiting a long while to tell you this.

51. Unless the boy stops talking, the master will punish him.

52. Do not do this if you wish to please me.

53. I deny having met your father in the town.

54. Agathōn did not deny having done the deed.

55. When he asked me that question I gave him no answer.

56. I will not depart before I have conquered.

57. The slave would not come before his master ordered him.

58. The army fetched provisions before the general came.

59. Major est injuria *quam ut* (eam) facile patiamur.

60. He asked me to give him money whenever I came to Athens.

61. He refused to go away unless I gave him the money.

62. I say that if you fight well you will conquer.

63. He said that if the men fought well they would conquer.

64. Knowing *that you were* busy, I did not like to come in.

V.

65. I am ashamed of having betrayed my country.

66. The Greeks were ashamed to desert Cyrus when in danger.

67. If you hurt my friend, you hurt me also.

68. He gave the Persians all Mēdia to inhabit.

69. A man is coming here to see me to-morrow.

70. A man cannot have all he wants, at least in this life.

71. My brother *was beforehand with* me in finishing that task.

72. What do you mean? I do not know what you mean.

73. I thought I had never seen a finer house than this.

74. It is hard to say which of these two boys is the more industrious.

75. You will never persuade me that you are telling the truth.

76. Callicli persuasum est ut Athenas iret.

77. Tu, si potuisses, id fecisses ; ego faciam si potero.

78. The rest of the citizens were left to protect the town.

79. I know that this man is not trustworthy.

80. He came into the house *without my knowing it.*

VI.

81. If you do not do what I bid you, you will repent it.

82. Sōcrates was too wise easily to get angry.

83. Tell me, stranger, what is your name and who is your father?

84. You are surely not so foolish as to trust Critias.

85. Some men eat to live, others live only to eat.

86. I was afraid you might meet my brother in the town.

87. What does it matter to us who will be king of Persia?

88. Nobody, as far as I know, ever said any such thing.

89. As soon as you have done what I ask you, I will go away.

90. I am not *the sort of person to* endure so great an insult.

91. If I tell you this, perhaps you will not believe me.

92. Is there any man *in the world* who knows all things?

93. Somebody perchance might say that you have acted unwisely.

94. I am afraid my father will not live many years longer.

95. *After the capture of* Milētus many of the citizens were put to death.

96. The foe that submits the victors ought to spare.

VII.

97. I say that the man who has done this thing is a coward and a villain.

98. Though all men despise Timōn, yet will not I.

99. Wait here for me, till I have returned from Athens.

100. I asked him how far Athens was from Thebes.

101. He replied that he did not know *what the distance was*.

102. Did I not forbid you to go out to-day?

103. Do you not understand how much you have yet to learn?

104. He begged me to tell him if my father was at home.

105. Leges patriae, si sapis, non violabis.

106. After murdering his younger brother he fled from Syracuse.

107. I entreated him to pity Damasippus *in his misfortunes*.

108. Do you know the man's name and of what country he is?

109. If he had intended to depart, he should have told me sooner.

110. See that you act not unfairly in this matter.

111. Whether this be true or false I care not at all.

112. When I return home I will tell you all that I have seen.

VIII.

113. If you do me this service, I will give you a reward.

114. If anyone were to ask me such a question I would not answer him.

115. If I had known this sooner I should not have come hither.

116. He told me that Xenicles, *with eight others*, was here to-day.

117. I am come to tell you what I heard from my father.

118. You cannot do whatever you choose here.

119. I shall be glad to see your sister when she arrives.

120. Whenever I see you doing wrong I will reprove you.

121. If the boy has disobeyed his father he must be punished.

122. *Had it not been for* my friends, I should have become very poor.

123. Ask the general himself what he intends to do.

124. What shall we do with a slave who runs away from his master?

125. If he should be caught he must not *get off unpunished.*

126. We should never forsake our friends because they are poor.

127. I congratulate you on having won a valuable prize.

128. If you took more pains, you might become wiser even than your masters.

IX.

129. In order to become truly wise, we must practise virtue.

130. He said he had not met Agathōn for two days.

131. I asked him how much money he had in his purse.

132. Unless Xenophōn comes quickly to the rescue, we are undone.

133. Would that I had been with you before Callias came!

134. Do not give me trouble, unless you wish to suffer.

135. Quis est *quin* intelligat solem luna esse majorem?

136. It is impossible for a river to flow upward from its source.

137. I do not know whether what you say is true or false.

138. It is uncertain whether my brother will be here to-day.

139. Clearchus has given orders that no one is to leave the camp.

140. Happy is *the man that* has never wasted a single day.

141. Even if you strike me, I shall not be angry with you.

142. Valere non potes, nisi corpus exercueris.

143. The Greeks were surprised that Cyrus did not make his appearance.

144. Take care the enemy do not surprise you unawares.

X.

145. King Archelaus sent for Sōcrates the philosopher, bidding him come to him.

146. There was such a fog that we could not see the enemy approaching.

147. As soon as the generals were assembled, it was resolved to summon the five captains.

148. I am aware that you consider yourself hardly treated by me.

149. Agēsilaus always praised those whom he saw marching orderly.

150. I went away early yesterday, so that I did not meet my friend.

151. If Empedocles had really been a god, he would surely not have died.

152. The boy very soon perceived that his master was not well pleased.

153. I told him very plainly that I would not suffer this.

154. If you (*pl.*) had not been here, we should have gone away long ago.

155. Beware of doing yourself what you forbid your children to do.

156. Dic mihi utrum noctes hieme an aestate breviores sint.

157. The gnat told the lion that he was not afraid of him.

158. While the shepherd slept, the wolf devoured the sheep.

159. Tell me who you are and what you have been doing.

160. Let no one suppose that I will betray my country.

XI.

161. Sunt qui credant lunam caseum esse.

162. Thinking that I should never persuade you (*pl.*), I stopped speaking.

163. Not only did he injure his friend, but he also insulted him.

164. Not only have you done me no good, but you have even done me harm.

165. I fear it may not be right to do this.

166. I have a right to punish the boy if he is idle.

167. Will you not forbear to commit so great an injustice ?

168. Were you to ask me for this, perhaps I should not give it you.

169. You are not the sort of man to be thus treated.

170. This being the case, we need say nothing more.

171. *So far from* blaming my conduct he even approved it.

172. You will have to learn much if you want to be wise.

173. Unless I am mistaken, your father will be here to-day.

174. Do not come to me before I call you.

175. Memini *me* ex patre meo hoc *audiisse.*

176. Memento me quoque mortalem *esse.*

XII.

177. Some say the men *of the present day* are better than their fathers.

178. As soon as you have finished that work, you may go out.

179. I cannot understand this, unless you explain it to me.

180. If I should see Critias, I will give him the money.

181. We were considering how many men we should leave behind us.

182. If anyone is caught running away, the truce will be at an end.

183. You are yet too young to understand such a difficult subject.

184. Let us finish our dinner before taking measures about the prisoners.

185. I should be foolish, were I not to do as you advise me.

186. What hinders my leaving Athens to-morrow?

187. The enemy may come upon us unawares, unless we are cautious.

188. Who is so ignorant as not to know this?

189. Can you not foresee what is going to happen now?

190. You should never be afraid of telling the truth.

191. He asked me if I knew the man we saw yesterday.

192. You cannot prevent me from saying what I wish in this matter.

XIII.

193. What is it that your father has given you, that you are so pleased?

194. I was much surprised at hearing you say this.

195. It is not your business to tell me what I should do.

196. Do not pretend to know what you do not understand.

197. If you know what is right, why do you not practise it?

198. *Without practising* virtue no one can become virtuous.

199. What a man you are to do everything so cleverly!

200. I request you to be ready when I come.

201. He said that he would be ready whenever I came.

202. *If* you do not obey (*part.*) the laws you will be punished.

203. Xenocleides, *since* he did not obey (*part.*) the magistrates, was put to death.

204. Phyllida amo, quamvis parva sit corpore.

205. Milo was so strong that he could carry an ox on his shoulders.

206. I would gladly do this, if you would help me.

207. I should not like to be *in that man's power* when he is angry.

208. After launching the ship, we set sail and proceeded in the direction of Salamis.

XIV.

209. I gave you the money on condition of your using it well.

210. Jupiter bade Deucalion ask for whatever he wanted.

211. If I must do this, I shall do it better *without your assistance.*

212. He came and told Nicias that he intended to sail away on the morrow.

213. I will give you this axe to cut down your trees with.

214. They all denied that you were the man who had done this.

215. I don't know what may happen, if he finds me here.

216. When I arrived at Athens, I found my brother waiting for me.

217. When they had come to close quarters the soldiers drew their swords.

218. If I had only seen you sooner, all this would not have occurred.

219. I cannot tell you how grateful I am for your kindness.

220. You need never be at a loss where to go.

221. I should like to know how many birds there are, and of what sort.

222. They asked me what induced you to leave the town.

223. I always feared his coming to some harm.

224. Seven times already have I told you not to be idle.

XV.

225. Critias wishes to be thought a wise man, *though he is not* one.

226. If Critias thinks he is wise, *when he is not*, what shall we call him?

227. I fear I am not clever enough to teach you all you want to learn.

228. A man cannot *be too soon about* getting himself a good wife.

229. Ought you not then to abstain from actions of this sort?

230. 'I am not so sure about that,' replied Aristippus.

231. Tell me plainly what sort of friends you would like to have.

232. If you spend all you earn, you will have nothing to give away.

233. Who knows whether his son will turn out wise or foolish?

234. Sōcrates asked Euthydēmus what was the difference between an intemperate man and a beast.

235. If you want to know what virtue really is, try to practise it.

236. Sōcrates was accused of saying that the sun was a stone and the moon earth.

237. Try, if you can, Critobūlus, to be a brave man.

238. We all love the man who is foremost to do a good action.

239. How this can be brought to pass I cannot imagine.

240. If fighting is needed, what will be the use of philosophy?

XVI.

241. I am not sure whether I ought to have done this or not.

242. *It is a true saying* that no man is at all times wise.

243. Before I saw the boy I could not tell what was the matter with him.

244. Should anyone say that a king need not obey the laws, he would speak falsely.

245. There is *a wonderful difference* between rashness and courage.

246. You evidently do not know as much as you think you do.

247. Do you think I would punish a boy who was trying *his best* to learn? not I.

248. If I wanted a true friend, where must I go to find him?

249. The more you try to persuade a donkey to proceed, the less he will obey you.

250. I am afraid Clearchus does not manage his soldiers as he ought.

251. I asked him if the house he had bought was to his liking.

252. Cleōn was not well pleased *at his friends being* so prosperous.

253. I should be glad to hear how you got on at Athens yesterday.

254. If he had meant to do this at all, he should have done it sooner.

255. He asked me why no one ever trusted him.

256. I replied, 'You are not the sort of man for anyone to trust.'

XVII.

257. I am in doubt whether to tell you this or not.

258. Singing loud is not the same thing as singing well.

259. I told him that if he did so I should blame him.

260. The master has told the boys twice already not to talk.

261. If they continue talking, they will be punished presently.

262. There are some who think wine is better than water.

263. But I am not sure whether water is not better than wine.

264. I will not go away till you have promised to oblige me.

265. The slave fled for refuge into a temple, that he might not be caught and punished.

266. I asked why he stayed at home so long, *when he might* have gone abroad.

267. You shall *certainly not* go out to-day, if I can prevent it.

268. If I meet the doctor in the town, I will pay him his fee.

269. Unless I had been there myself, I could not have believed it possible.

270. I did not ask him what he intended to do.

271. Tell me quickly what I want to know.

272. It is not *my wish* that you should stay here all day.

XVIII.

273. Why were you not at home to welcome me?

274. He promised to come if ever I sent for him.

275. I did not clearly understand what the old man meant to say.

276. I will not stop speaking till I have persuaded you.

277. I did not know whether he was alive or dead.

278. Are you going to disobey me? *what folly !*

279. Edictum est militibus ne castris exirent.

280. If you are *mad enough to* do this, you will surely be punished.

281. The Greeks thought that if they chose Hēgēsander, they would be likely to prosper.

282. When Agias saw the boy running past, he caught hold of him by the left leg.

283. The soldiers asked Clearchus why they had to endure so many hardships.

284. If nothing prevents me, I will come directly after dinner.

285. He is too wise to be angry at so trifling a matter.

286. I have long been wishing to tell you how much I love you.

287. The better a man is the more men often hate him.

288. If anyone says this is true, I will not believe him.

XIX.

289. *In the hearing of* the people Cleōn spoke as follows.

290. Try to touch me *without my perceiving it.*

291. Do you not understand this, you who understand most things ?

292. It is of more importance what you are than who you are.

293. Beware of associating with evil companions.

294. This being the case, we need proceed no further.

295. There is no living pleasantly with such a wife as this.

296. So far from confessing his faults, he even denies them.

297. Do not be so foolish as to go up that mountain without a guide.

298. When I went yesterday to see him, he was not at home.

299. If I had caught you in the town, I would have sent you home again.

300. The enemy must be resisted if they attempt to cross the river.

301. I knew that if we fought we should prove victorious.

302. What you have sworn to do, you ought to do at once.

303. No one is so strong as not to be ill sometimes.

304. Though I suffer much I am not allowed to complain.

XX.

305. Beware of promising what you would be unable to perform.

306. Haec, sive recte sive male facta sunt, ego me fecisse confiteor.

307. Some men, if they suffered as much as I do, would think themselves badly treated.

308. See that you don't try to get along too fast.

309. Do you know if Agathocles surrendered of his own accord?

310. The vessel is said to have sunk *when at a little distance* from land.

311. About the same time that you passed my house I was standing in the street.

312. I asked him what was *the nature and extent* of his dominions.

313. If Eumenes persists in *this course of action*, I shall ask him what *the result* is likely to be.

314. Surely they will never be so foolish as to prefer war to peace.

315. *There is no saying* what he may do *under provocation.*

316. Do you know that if you strive after virtue you will be happy all your life?

317. Why did they condemn Xanthippus to death without knowing the truth?

318. Should he charge me with folly, there is no one who would believe him.

319. You seem to me to be quite at a loss what to say.

320. We hear that you have succeeded in this matter beyond your expectations.

XXI.

321. After besieging the town four months, Lamachus took it, *inhabitants and all.*

322. I am told that about seven hundred men marched up the hill last night.

323. Nothing could ever prevent Callistratus from doing what he deemed to be right.

324. How is it that you are so clever at finding fault with others?

325. Before reaching my father's house you will have to cross the river.

326. I would not take so much pains merely to oblige Amynias.

327. Am I then to be taught wisdom by a little boy *like you?*

328. You all look at me, as if you expected to hear something wonderful.

329. Why do you prefer to live so miserably, *when you might* lead a happy life?

330. I knew that if you were *in my place,* you would do the same as I am doing.

331. You need not have come so far to tell me this old story.

332. Do you suppose that Sōcrates ever acted impiously or unjustly?

333. I promise that if I ever return safe home, I will reward you.

334. He would never have concealed this from me, unless he had had good reason for it.

335. He ought to be ashamed of himself, if he does not learn wisdom.

336. He used to wait about the house about daybreak, till the door was opened.

XXII.

337. After Charicles had spoken, all the people applauded.

338. Hannibal, si quis alius, bello erat peritus.

339. If that is the case, we will go to Ephesus in a few days.

340. He came home to dinner, although no one expected *his return.*

341. It is not proper to bathe when the water is so cold.

342. Where we shall go this summer we do not yet know.

343. Whenever he came home late, he went to bed without supper.

344. I would never believe him to be a thief, unless he were caught stealing.

345. He sent me to tell you not to give these men any answer.

346. Omnes precantur deos ut mala a se avertant.

347. I shall remain here only on condition that you keep me company.

348. It so happened that not one of the generals was present *on that occasion.*

349. What have I done to deserve to be thus treated?

350. I should be very much pleased if you would grant me what I ask.

351. How is it that you *take so long a time* to learn a few things?

352. How hard it is for a man, who wishes to mind his own business, to live at Athens!

XXIII.

353. We must all try as much as we can to learn what is good for us.

354. What would you say of a man who never *called* the same thing *by the same name?*

355. Quisnam Cratippum impediet, quominus Athenas redeat?

356. If you do me a kindness, be sure you will get gratitude in return.

357. Thus having bidden each other farewell, each went his own way.

358. He seems to be at a loss, and not to know how to begin his speech.

359. I should certainly invite many friends to dinner, whenever I offered a sacrifice.

360. It is *the height of* folly to use for our hurt what was made for our benefit.

361. Sōcrates believed that nothing could ever escape the knowledge of the Gods.

362. If you are not hungry or thirsty, do not force yourself to eat and drink.

363. If the Lesbians want more money, let them send ships to obtain it.

364. Although Chaerephōn is an old man, he still serves in the army.

365. Who would have thought that the city would have surrendered within ten days?

366. The little boy, not knowing what to do with the bird, began to cry.

367. Cleōn then departed, promising to perform all that he had undertaken.

368. The mother proceeded to ask me which of her two daughters I thought the fairest.

XXIV.

369. That this is possible I admit, but whether it be prudent is another matter.

370. If you had trusted that man more, you would have got what you wanted long ago.

371. I am afraid that no one is likely to *take you for* a poet.

372. We told Amynias to send word as soon as ever he arrived at Ephesus.

373. I asked him what there was to prevent me leaving Athens immediately.

374. The Lacedaemonians have taken up arms to recover some towns formerly belonging to them.

375. A man of your age ought to have known that the water was too cold for bathing.

376. They carried out their intentions as far as they could, but it was impossible to effect all that they desired.

377. There was not a man, save Leōtychides himself, that escaped being put to death.

378. He asked me what on earth led me to believe that you had done this deed.

379. So long as my fortune lasted I lived in luxury.

380. But now that I have spent my money, I am forced to live sparingly.

381. I could not have supposed Speusippus to be guilty of theft, had he not confessed it himself.

382. They then marched straight for the town, not being in the least aware of what had happened.

383. Sōcratem capitis damnaverunt Athenienses, *quod contempsisset* deos.

384. Orders were given to start on the following day, and make for the nearest town.

XXV.

385. What do you think will become of us now that we have lost our leader?

386. The soldiers were much distressed at not having sufficient money for the journey.

387. When the men were brought before Cleander, he asked them what they had seen.

388. If we have no hope of *success in the future,* what will be the use of going further?

389. The army had orders to be ready to march, as soon as the signal was given.

390. Sōcrates once asked a commander why Homer called Agamemnon the 'shepherd of the people.'

391. Meanwhile the generals held a council *upon the question of* continuing their march inland.

392. The soldiers agreed, that if anyone went out foraging on his own account, *the proceeds* should be public property.

393. We all agreed that Chaerephōn was the most troublesome person we had ever met with.

394. If *the whole city* had acted as you have done, we should not now be in difficulties.

395. How do you suppose I can compel him to accompany me, if he does not like?

396. Tissaphernes promised to lead the army to a place where they might get plenty of provisions.

397. Xanthippus found fault with his son for not asking for whatever he wanted.

398. Imperator milites hortatus est ut vallum struerent, arma caperent, se suaque defenderent.

399. Permultum sane interest, quales sint imperatores nostri quam qui sint.

400. Quis dixit, non aurum habere sibi praeclarum videri, sed iis qui haberent imperare?

THIRD PART.

I.

Xenophōn with his two hundred cavalry arrived at Tyriaeum, having now (ἤδη) marched more than thirteen stadia through Lydia and Phrygia. Here he met Epyaxa, the wife of Syennesis, king of Cilicia, and, *in order to* please her, he made (*middle*) a review of his whole army. But when the queen saw the Greek soldiers charging *at full speed*, she feared greatly and cried out. The barbarians also fled to their tents *in much alarm* [1].

II.

They therefore without, as had been agreed, gave the signal, and one of the sentinels from the wall answered them; then they ran immediately *to those places in which* [2] they had been ordered to set the ladders. But by some accident the other sentinel was not upon his own part of the wall, so that when the ladder was placed there (*gen. abs.*) a soldier cried out, that he might get help.

III.

Some of the cavalry then rode up and told Agēsilaus that there were eighty of the enemy's soldiers hidden under the temple, and asked him what they should do. And Agesilaus, although he [3] *was severely wounded*, did not forget the deity, but ordered them to let the enemy go and not to injure them.

[1] Use a participle with adverb.　　　[2] Say 'thither where.'
[3] Say ' had many wounds.'

IV.

Melaniōn then with his eight thousand marched through Phrygia and Cilicia, and came to the confines of Syria. But as the enemy nowhere appeared, he ascended a certain hill to view the country *which lay*[1] below. Through the plain flowed the river Pyramus, and between the hill and the river there was not a single house or tree. Beyond the river the enemy's camp extended four stades in length, and guards were stationed at every gate. The rest of the army remained within the camp, some sitting by the fires, others slowly pacing to and fro. All, as it seemed, were ready[2] *for an engagement* on that same day, or at least upon the morrow. But the king himself was not visible, nor did Melanion know where he was. Presently a messenger rode up *with the news* that the king's force was very near-at-hand.

V.

After this Leōtychides the Megarian obtained the kingdom, and one son was born to him named Zeuxidēmus. This son however was never king of Sparta, for he died before his father, leaving one child Archidēmus. When Leotychides had lost Zeuxidemus he married a second wife, by whom he had no son but a daughter only.

VI.

Idathyrsus, king of the Scythians, against whom Darius was marching, tried to persuade the Ionian chiefs to free themselves by breaking down the bridge over the Danube. *When they refused*, because of their promise to Darius, he called them slaves and cowards.

[1] Do not use a relative pronoun.   [2] ὡς with fut. part.

VII.

Lysimachus, having been conquered in Thrace, and forced to surrender himself and his army for want of water, afterwards exclaimed (as he was) drinking, 'For (ἕνεκα) what a small gratification have I made myself a slave.'

VIII.

Now Tachybūlus, seeing that his men were weak for want of food, desired to relieve them; so, having found a certain man of Boeōtia, who said that villages were near, whence they might get provisions for the army, he proclaimed that all *who desired it* might go for (ἐπὶ) the provisions. And hearing this two thousand men immediately went out from-among the soldiers. But while they were in the villages and were taking the provisions, the enemy's cavalry, seeing the Greeks plundering, fell upon them, and slew of them not fewer than five hundred. Besides these, more than eight hundred are said to have been taken prisoners.

IX.

The rest of the Greeks then fled to the mountains; and hereupon a messenger came running very fast and reported the matter to Xenophōn, who at once proceeded to succour the men, and seventy chosen warriors with him. These recovered *the fugitives*, and brought them back to the camp in safety. By this time night was coming on, and some of the Mysian cavalry suddenly attacked the rear of the Greeks, slaying some and pursuing the remainder as far as the camp. Whereupon the Greeks ran at once to (ἐπὶ) their arms, but they thought it not safe to pursue the enemy in the dark, so they passed the whole night *on guard*.

X.

Then Orontes coming to Cyrus at Sittacē told him all *that had happened.* Cyrus however said, 'I will not be a judge for you (*pl.*) in such matters; but go, tell the king that I will be with him on this very day.' So Orontes departed, taking with him four thousand heavy-armed and a thousand cavalry, and marching through the plain they came on the third day to the river Euphrates, which is very deep and broad in that place. And in this district provisions were plentiful; so the army took much corn and barley and wine, and oil in jars, and they feasted there for thirteen days *with good cheer.* Thus everything turned out as they desired.

XI.

When Agathocles was besieging a certain city, some soldiers on the walls insulted him saying, 'Son of a potter, whence will you get pay for your soldiers?' He answered smiling, 'I shall take your city and give it to them.' After a few days he took the city by storm; then, having sold the prisoners as slaves, he gained a large sum of money.

XII.

Since this seemed to the Thebans to be the best advice, they straightway sent and asked the people of Aegina to help them, *as they were* their kinsmen. The Aeginētans, pleased at the request and remembering their old grudge against the Athenians, at once began war without proclamation. Sailing off in their men of war, they ravaged Phalērum and many other places along the shore, and (by) so doing greatly injured the Athenians.

XIII.

They say that Niobē (while) still alive was turned into a stone on the tomb of her children. But whoever believes that a woman was formed out of a stone or a stone out of a woman is a simpleton. The truth is as follows. Niobe, when her children died, made a stone image and set it up on their tomb; therefore this story is told about her.

XIV.

Thence, *after feasting*, they advanced eight stadia, and came to a beautiful city, where they saw men women and children rejoicing exceedingly. A great battle had taken place, and the enemy, *after many had been slain*, was defeated. The victor with his soldiers happened *to be* present; many *were* the honours *which*[1] the people bestowed upon him. Great was the joy, but greater still was the gratitude of the survivors, for *in those days* men who were defeated in battle suffered terrible things at-the-hands-of (πρὸς *with gen.*) their conquerors.

XV.

Once an old man having cut some wood (*pl.*) was carrying it on his shoulders along the road. Tired with the weight of his burden, he threw away the wood and called for Death. Death then straightway appearing asked him what he wanted. Then the old man replied, 'I want you to put this load again upon my shoulders.'

XVI.

The guards happened not to be at the gate when Xenias came running up; so he shouted to the men inside the town to summon some fresh sentinels to their post. But they did

---

[1] See note 1, p. 44.

not understand clearly what he said (φθέγγομαι), and no one came *at his bidding.* Then Xenias got very angry, and taking off his helmet, which was of brass and very heavy, he threw it *with all his might* into the face of the nearest man inside the gates. But this happened to be not a soldier at all, but a quiet harmless old man, who had come up hearing the noise, and was just putting his head outside the gate to see what was the matter. So this old man was much surprised (at) receiving what he by no means expected.

XVII.

A herdsman who was tending a herd of cattle once lost a calf. He then went through all the district and spent his time (in) looking for it. After some time he prayed to Zeus to show him the robber *who stole* the calf, saying that he would sacrifice a kid to him. Next day, as he was walking through a wood, he found a lion eating the calf. Being greatly frightened he lifted up his hands to heaven and prayed, saying, ' O lord Zeus, if only I escape from this lion, I will sacrifice a bull to thee.'

XVIII.

Scilūrus left behind him many children. Now when he was about to die, he gave each boy a bundle of javelins and ordered them to break it. All having tried in vain to break the bundle, he himself took out the javelins one by one and broke them all easily. ' This,' said he, ' teaches you that you will keep strong (by) standing together, but that if you quarrel you will become weak.'

XIX.

After the victory *was won,* the Greek generals held a meeting about the *distribution of* the spoil, intending to give the largest portion to the one who should appear most worthy of it. It was likewise determined to name the second in order, that he also might receive the honour that was due to him. But when the votes were taken (ψῆφους τίθεσθαι) each man was found to have assigned the first prize to himself, while all had given the second to Themistocles. So for a long time they were at a loss what to do, all being equal; but at last Themistocles, finding himself to be second *in the estimation of* the others, but first *in his own*, claimed to receive the largest share of the spoil.

XX.

Once *during a heavy fall of* snow, a stranger asked one of the Scythian chieftains whether he was cold, seeing that he went about naked. The Scythian asked the stranger in return if his face was cold; and when the other replied *in the negative*, he said, 'No more am I, for I am all face.'

XXI.

During the Persian war the Athenians, fearing for their safety, determined to abandon their city, and conveying their wives and children to Troezēn, to go on board their ships and fight for the liberty of Greece by sea. But *one* Cyrsilus proposed that they should remain at Athens and admit Xerxes into the city. Thereupon the citizens enraged at his cowardice stoned Cyrsilus to death, as a traitor to his country.

XXII.

Cadmus is said to have slain a dragon at Dircē, and to have sown its teeth in the same district. From these teeth it was said that armed men sprang up. But the true story is as follows. Cadmus, a Phoenician by birth, came to Thebes to

E

his brother to contend for the sovereignty. Amongst his possessions he had a number of elephant's teeth. Now the king of the Thebans was named Draco, whom Cadmus slew and became king in his stead. Then the friends of Draco fought against Cadmus, and having plundered his goods stole the teeth. After this they fled and were scattered in different directions (ἄλλοι ἀλλαχῇ). Starting again from these places they made war upon the Thebans, and since they had stolen the teeth the Thebans said, 'Cadmus has brought upon us these misfortunes, having slain Draco, and from his (ἐκείνου) teeth many fierce warriors have risen up to fight against us.'

XXIII.

The cavalry then dispersing began to set everything on fire wherever they went, and the peltasts marching abreast of them along the heights, burnt whatever they found combustible. The main body too did the same, if they found anything left behind by the others, so that the whole country seemed to be on fire, and the Greek force to be very numerous. As soon as it was time (ὥρα) they mounted a hill and encamped. When they *caught sight of* the enemy's fires, about five miles distant, they themselves then lighted as many fires as they could.

As soon as they had had supper *the order was given* to put out all the fires, and having stationed sentinels, they lay down to sleep. At daybreak, having prayed to the Gods and arrayed themselves for battle, they continued their march *with the greatest possible speed*. Timasiōn and the cavalry, taking the guides and riding forward, reached the top of the hill where the Greeks were besieged, but saw no troops there. This they reported to Xenophōn, wondering what *could have happened*.

XXIV.

In the following year Lysander again commanded the navy, although it was contrary to custom that the same man should be twice admiral. He sailed to Lampsacus, and since he *was first to* arrive, prevented the Athenians from saving the town, which soon surrendered to him. Then having waited until the Athenian sailors had left their ships to obtain provisions, he quickly captured as many as he could and gave chase to the remainder.

XXV.

Diogenes once, when washing vegetables, laughed at Aristippus as he passed by, saying, 'If you had learnt to eat vegetables, you would not have been a slave in the court of a tyrant.' Aristippus replied, 'If you had known how to behave among men, you would not now have been washing vegetables.' Once when Dionysius asked him why the philosophers haunt the doors of the rich, while the rich do not frequent those of the philosophers, he said, 'Because the former know what they want, but the latter do not.'

XXVI.

The frogs, distressed because they had no king, sent envoys to Zeus to ask him to provide one for them. The father of the gods, perceiving their simplicity, smiled and threw down a log into the water. The frogs, alarmed at the noise, hid themselves by diving to the bottom of the lake. After some time one of them chanced to lift up his head above the water, and after examining the log-of-wood summoned the rest. Soon finding that the log remained motionless, they swam up to it, and leaping upon it sat there, insulting it *in every possible way.* Then they *sent another message* to Zeus, saying that the king he had sent was useless. The god then being angry sent a water-snake, by which they were all seized and devoured. This fable teaches us to submit to present misfortunes, lest greater evils come upon us.

XXVII.

When Xerxes was marching against Greece he was magnificently entertained at Celaenae, by one Pythius. Xerxes asked him how much money he had, and thanked him greatly for his hospitality. Pythius, highly gratified at this, proceeded to ask a favour of the king. He said that his five sons were about to serve in the Persian army, and prayed that the eldest might be allowed to remain at home to support him *in his old age.* 'What!' said Xerxes, 'dost thou dare to talk to me about thy son, when I myself am on the march with all the relatives and friends that I have?' He then gave orders that the eldest son, *whose life* Pythius had desired to save, should be instantly put to death.

XXVIII.

A few days afterwards Solōn met a stranger who said that he had lately come from Athens. When Solon asked him if he had any news to tell, the man, as he was taught, said, ' Nothing, except that a young man is dead, the son of a certain nobleman, whom all the citizens honoured, and who is now abroad.' 'Who would not pity the father,' said Solon, ' whoever he may be? But what is his name?' 'I do not remember,' said the stranger, ' although I have heard it. They said that he was very just and wise.' Solon, fearing very much lest it should be his own son who was dead, asked whether it was Solon's name he had heard; and when the stranger said that it was, he *burst into tears*, beat his head, and said such things as wretched men are wont (φιλέω) to say. Afterwards however it appeared that the story was not true.

XXIX.

Once a farmer had a fat goose, which was stolen from him. So he went and complained to the priest, desiring him to recover the goose for him, if he could. The priest promised to try. So the next day, when all the people were assembled, he went up to the pulpit, as though he would address them, and bade everyone sit down. When they had all *taken their seats*, he said, 'Why don't you all sit down?' 'We are all sitting ready,' they cried. 'Nay' (ἀλλά), said the priest, 'the *man who stole* the goose is not sitting.' '*Yes, I am*,' exclaimed the thief. 'Say you so?' replied the priest; 'then I charge you to take the goose back again immediately.'

XXX.

After Hēracles was taken up to heaven, his sons fleeing from Eurystheus came to Athens, and sitting down at the altar of Zeus craved assistance. Eurystheus bade the Athenians surrender the fugitives, threatening war; but they refused to give them up, preferring to decide the matter by conflict. The sons of Eurystheus were slain in the battle, and the king himself took to flight. Hyllus pursued and captured Eurystheus; he slew him and cut off his head, and sent it to Alcmēna, the mother of Heracles, *who* bored out the eyes of Eurystheus with a pin.

XXXI.

We are told that when Croesus heard what the men of Lampsacus had done, he sent them a letter, bidding them surrender Miltiades. They hesitated for some time what to

do, for Croesus had threatened that he would destroy them
'like (τρόπον) a pine-tree.' They therefore consulted one of
the soothsayers as to what this saying might mean. He
replied, 'The pine-tree is the only one which, when once cut
down, never puts forth any more branches, but perishes
utterly.' Alarmed at these words, the men were afraid of
what Croesus might do to them, and accordingly gave up
Miltiades.

XXXII.

Dēmosthenes and Eurymedon, as soon as the Thūrians
had prepared to join them with as large a force as they could
muster, ordered their ships to coast along until they came to
Crotōn. They themselves having first reviewed their land
forces on the banks of the river Sybaris, marched through the
Thurian territory. Now when they reached the river Hylias,
the people of Croton sent and told them that they would not
allow the army to pass through their country. They therefore encamped by the sea at the mouth of the river, where
their vessels met them. On the following day they put all
their men on board and coasted along, touching at all the
towns except Locri, till they arrived at Petra.

XXXIII.

One day the king lost his way in the forest and came to a
poor man's cottage unknown. After supper the man and
his wife began to talk about the king, saying that in most
respects he was a good man, but that he often neglected his
friends, because he was so fond of hunting. The king did not
say anything at the time, but went away. Next day at
sunrise he rode up to the cottage accompanied by his
guards (δορυφόροι). As he wore his purple robe and crown
he was easily recognised, and he then spoke as follows:

'Since the day when I began to reign, I have never heard any true words about myself until I saw you and your wife yesterday.'

XXXIV.

As soon as Aristeides saw them, he advanced a long way before his troops, and calling out with a loud voice, conjured them by the gods of their country, ' to abandon this impious war and not to oppose the Athenians, who were hastening to aid the men that were now risking their lives for the safety of Greece.' Finding however that *instead of listening* to him they advanced in a hostile manner, he *quitted his design* of going to help the Lacedaemonians, and began to fight with these Greeks, the greater part of whom presently gave way and retreated.

XXXV.

The Athenians then sent Dēmosthenes to Sicily with sixty-five ships, and as many men as he could obtain from each state. He first of all landed in Laconia, and having ravaged some of the land, fortified a spot opposite the island of Cythēra. He then sailed along the coast towards Corcyra, in order to take up some of the allies there. On his way thither he was met by Eurymedon, who was now returning from Sicily, for he had been sent there in the winter with money for the troops. When they had consulted together, they determined to send ten ships at once to help Conon, the commander at Naupactus.

XXXVI.

Once there was a very thoughtless man named Melanion, who had a house. Overtaken by poverty (for he had formerly been very rich), he was compelled to sell it. So he put on

his cloak and started for the market-place, where a great
many people used to come together every day. When he
arrived he explained *his business* to those sitting around. It
happened there was present a stranger who proposed to buy
himself a house in that town. Therefore, after asking many
questions about the house of Melanion, he said that he desired
to see it, in order that after investigation he might either take
it or let it go. Thereupon the other said, 'What need of that?
See! I have with me something which is a proof *of the
excellent building of* the house.' Thus saying he displayed a
brick which he was carrying hidden in his cloak. All laughed
so loudly that the foolish man retired *without effecting his
purpose.*

XXXVII.

Thence we sailed to Ceōs, and remaining there for nine
days because the wind was contrary, on the tenth in the
evening (*gen.*) we weighed anchor and arrived next morning
at Dēlos. Now the Delians were troubled at that time with
a pestilential kind of malady. They *had white* (*leprosy*)[1] on
their faces and their hair turned white. They supposed that
this had happened to them in consequence of the anger of
Apollo. Thereupon we made our escape from this island as
soon as possible, sailing away in the night, for fear lest some
one of us might catch the same complaint.

XXXVIII.

Upon this Alexander rode forward in front of the line with
a few companions and met Pōrus. Pulling up his horse he
greatly admired Porus, because he did not appear at all downcast in spirit, but came to meet him like a brave man who
had fought valiantly for his kingdom. Alexander then first

---

[1] Say 'they were infected with white.'

asked him to say what he desired for himself. They say that Porus answered, 'Treat me like a king, Alexander.' Pleased at this request Alexander answered, 'This shall be *your lot*, Porus, for my sake; now therefore tell me what you would like on your own account.' Porus replied that he wished for nothing besides. Alexander then was still more pleased at his words, and gave him more territory than he had before, and always for the future treated him as a friend.

XXXIX.

Meanwhile the general sent forward a hundred picked men, that as soon as any gates were opened they might be the first to rush in. These after waiting some time had come by degrees near the town, while the party within, having opened the gates *leading to* (κατὰ) the market-place by cutting through the bar, brought round a number of men to the postern-gate, in order by a sudden attack to terrify the townsmen, knowing nothing of what was going on. Next they raised the appointed signal, which when the general observed he ordered his men to rush forward with a shout. Thereupon some immediately rushed in through the gates, others over some square planks that happened to be lying by the wall, which had fallen down and was now being rebuilt. *This movement* caused the greatest consternation to those within, and the greater part of the soldiers turned immediately upwards into the higher quarters of the town, desiring to take the citadel; the rest of the multitude spread themselves in all directions.

XL.

Boges, who was governor of Eïon in Thrace, at the time when Xerxes was marching against Greece, is deemed worthy of great commendation. For when he was besieged by the Athenians under Cimōn, the son of Miltiades, and might have retired from the city on stated conditions (ἐπὶ ῥητοῖς) and returned into Asia, he refused to do so, lest the king should think he had saved his own life through cowardice. Therefore instead of surrendering he held out to the last. And when there was no longer any food in the fortress, he raised a great funeral pile, slew his children, his wife, and his servants, and cast them all into the fire. Then collecting all the gold and silver that was in the city, he flung it from the walls into the river Strymōn; this done, he threw himself upon the burning pile. For this Boges is justly praised by the Persians even to this day.

XLI.

The Corinthians then sent envoys to the Athenians, who spoke as follows: 'Ye do wrong, Athenians, in beginning war and breaking treaties; for while we are avenging ourselves upon our enemies, ye stand in our way and take up arms against us. Now if your purpose is to prevent us from sailing to Corcyra or elsewhere, and if you wish to break the treaty, first seize us who are here and deal with us as enemies.' The Corcyraeans who heard this exclaimed, ' Seize them and put them to death!' But the Athenians replied as follows: 'We are neither beginning war nor breaking the treaties; but we are come to aid the people of Corcyra, who are our allies. If therefore you desire to sail in any other direction, we shall not stand in your way; but if you are intending to sail against Corcyra or to any of the places belonging to the Corcyraeans, we shall prevent it as far as is in our power.' The Athenians having thus replied, the Corinthians began to prepare for their voyage homewards.

XLII.

Datis at this time was marching into Asia with his army, and while he was at Myconus he saw a vision in his sleep. What the vision was is not told us, but, as soon as it was day, he made an examination of the vessels; and having found in a Phoenician ship a gilded image of Apollo, he discovered that it had been stolen. The same day therefore he sailed off in his own ship to Dēlos to restore the image to the temple *to which it belonged*. Having reached the island he ordered the Delians to carry the image to Dēlium, which is a town of Boeōtia on the sea opposite Chalcis. After his departure however, the Delians did not obey his orders, but after an interval of twenty years the Thebans conveyed the image to Dēlium.

XLIII.

Thereupon the Scythian princes, knowing that the Persians were in great distress, sent a herald to the camp with presents for king Darius; a bird, a mouse, a frog, and five arrows. The Persians asked the messenger what the gifts might mean; he replied, however, that *his orders were merely* to deliver them and take his departure immediately. He bade the Persians, if they were wise, to discover the meaning for themselves. Accordingly they held a council, and after *various opinions had been given*, Gōbryas got up and spoke as follows: 'I for my part conjecture the matter thus. Unless ye can turn yourselves into birds and fly up into the sky, or burrow in the ground like mice, or become frogs and leap into the lakes, ye will never return home again, but die in this land, stricken (βάλλω) by the Scythian arrows.' Thus the Persians interpreted the gifts.

XLIV.

Themistocles then fled *under compulsion* to Corcyra. But the Corcyraeans, fearing to keep him and thus incur the enmity of the Athenians and Lacedaemonians, conveyed him over to the mainland. Thence he made his way to Ephesus, and having gone up the country with one of the Persians on the coast, he sent a letter to king Artaxerxes *in these terms:* ' I, Themistocles, have come to thee, who of all the Greeks have done most harm to your house, while I was compelled to defend myself against thy father; but who also did him far more good by preventing the Greeks from destroying the bridges over the Hellespont, when he was returning from Europe into Asia. And now I am here, able to do thee good service, being persecuted by the Greeks on account of my good-will to thee.' Artaxerxes, *we are told*, received him graciously, and in course of time, having learnt the Persian language, Themistocles was held in great repute by the king, and promised to make all Greece subject to him. But after-wards, finding himself unable to *fulfil his promise*, he is said to have *committed suicide* by poison.

XLV.

Once there was a king of Egypt, Rhampsinitus, who was the wealthiest of all the kings that reigned before or after him. Desiring to treasure up his riches in safety, he ordered a chamber of stone to be built for this purpose. The builder, however, so contrived it that one of the stones in the outer wall of this chamber should be removable *at pleasure. On his death-bed* he revealed the matter to his two sons, and showed them how they might remove the stone and possess themselves of the king's money. After their father's death the young men, *following his instructions*, entered the chamber by night and took away large quantities of gold and silver. When they had done this several times, the king perceiving that his treasure grew continually less, the doors of the chamber being all the while fast closed, he ordered traps to be set round the vessels in which the money was deposited. So when the thieves came as before, one of them entering was immediately caught (ἐνέχεσθαι) in a trap. *Finding escape impossible*, he called his brother and bade him cut off his head and carry it away with him, that he might not be recognised. The other did as he was told, and next day, when the king came and found a body in the trap without a head he was greatly astonished.

XLVI.

After these images were stolen, the Epidaurians ceased paying the tribute to Athens which they had agreed upon. The Athenians therefore sent envoys to demand it; but the Epidaurians replied that they were not doing any wrong, since as long as they had the images in their country they had fulfilled the agreement, but now that they were taken away it was not fair that they should still pay the tribute, but that the Athenians must demand it from the Aeginetans who now had the images. The Athenians therefore sent to Aegina and demanded the images themselves; whereupon the Aeginetans replied that they would not restore them. On hearing this the Athenians sent some vessels to Aegina to take the images by force.

XLVII.

The townsmen, finding that the enemy was within their walls, were much alarmed at first; but perceiving that their opponents were not very numerous, they thought that by a sudden attack they might easily overpower them. So they resolved to try; and when everything was in readiness, while it was still night they went out of their houses against the Thebans, and came to close quarters with them as quickly as they could. The enemy, deceived in their expectations, began to repel their attacks, and beat them off two or three times. But afterwards, when the men assailed them with loud shouts, the women screaming from the houses and pelting them with stones and tiles, a violent rain also having come on during the night, they were frightened and fled through the city; most of them being unacquainted with the streets, while their pursuers *knew them well* (ἔμπειρος εἶναι), so that they could not easily escape, and many were put to death. Being chased up and down the city, some climbed up the wall and throwing themselves over most of them perished; others came to a deserted gate, and having found an axe cut through the bar and thus got out unobserved, while many were cut down while scattered in different directions about the city.

XLVIII.

Now I happened to meet this man Callias the son of Hipponicus, who himself had two sons; so I questioned him, saying, 'Callias, if your sons had been colts or calves, I suppose you would have procured some one as a trainer for them, and such a man would have been accustomed to look after horses or cattle. But *as it is*, since they are men, whom do you intend to get as a master for them, for I suppose that you have considered this, since you have sons?' 'Of course I have,' said he. 'Who is he?' said I, 'of what country, and *what is his fee?*' 'Euēnus,' he replied, 'a Parian; *he charges five minae.'* Hearing this I thought Euenus a happy man indeed, if he really possessed this art.

XLIX.

I will now relate the story of this battle, for such another was never fought in our time. The soldiers under Agēsilaus advanced into the plain of Corōnea from the Cēphisus. whilst the Thebans came up from Mount Helicōn. For some time as they moved on there was a *deep silence* in the ranks on both sides, but when about a furlong distant from each other the Thebans shouted and rushed forward. When they came still nearer, that division of Agesilaus' army which Hērippidas commanded advanced to meet them, and coming to close quarters routed the line opposed to them. The Argives then did not wait for Agesilaus' own division, but fled to Mount Helicon. *The victory* however *was not very decisive*, but the Thebans acknowledged their defeat. Agesilaus then made his way to Sparta, where he was joyfully welcomed.

L.

When the banquet was ready, Seuthes went in with his Greek guests and they all sat down. Then tables were brought in loaded with meat, and beside the meat were placed huge loaves of bread. Seuthes first taking the loaf that lay beside him, broke it up *into small pieces* (κατὰ μικρόν) and tossed them to his guests, and the meat likewise. Now there was an Arcadian present, Arystas by name; he taking in his hand the largest loaf he could find, and placing a quantity of meat upon his knees, began his dinner. Next horns full of wine were carried round, from which everyone drank. But Arystas, when the horn was presented to him, exclaimed: ' Give yonder man the wine, for I have no leisure

yet.' Seuthes hearing the sound of his voice asked what he
had said, for he did not understand Greek. When this was
told him he laughed heartily, and so did the rest of the
company.

LI.

Gyges was a shepherd in the service of the king of Lydia.
One day, *after a violent storm of rain*, the ground was rent
asunder by an earthquake, and a chasm appeared on the
spot where Gyges was feeding his flock. Into this he
descended, and found a hollow brazen horse with windows in
its sides, through which he looked and saw a corpse of
superhuman size with a gold ring on its finger. This he
took off, and afterwards at a meeting of the shepherds
Gyges came with the rest, wearing the ring. As he sat with
his companions, he happened to turn the bezel of the ring
round to the inside of his hand: whereupon he became
invisible to the shepherds, and while marvelling at this he
turned the bezel to the outside again, and became once more
visible. *After this discovery* he contrived to be sent as one
of the messengers to the palace, and soon afterwards
conspired against the king and slew him. Thus by virtue of
this ring Gyges got possession of the throne.

LII.

In this manner the fight began, the king's forces pressing
with their utmost vigour up the hill along these four roads, and
the enemy as obstinately defending their own ground. The
fight continued doubtful till the middle of the afternoon.
Word was then brought to the chief officers of the Arcadians
that their expected allies would not arrive before the next
day. Concealing this news from the soldiers they determined

to advance to the top of the hill, so that they might be on even ground with the enemy, and in this the soldiers so *seconded the officers' courage and resolution* that they soon began to gain ground in every direction.

LIII.

Then having called together his soldiers, he at once told them that they must now fight with the greatest courage unless they wished their country to be enslaved by the tyrant. The gods [1] were evidently favourable to *their cause*, and would punish the lawless and impious. Let them therefore advance without fear, since *their small force* would not escape the notice of the enemy, who felt almost certain of victory.

LIV.

Next day at sunrise, before the enemy suspected our design, we began the retreat, hoping that, if we could only cross the river in safety, we should be able to escape unperceived. For some time the enemy *showed no sign*; slowly we moved across the plain towards the river, no one uttering a sound. We knew that there was only one boat moored to the bank on this side; this we determined to seize and so to cross the river. We had just reached the stream, but found *to our dismay* that only half our men could cross at one time. *Our first detachment* crossed the river in safety; but it seemed almost impossible that the rest could save themselves before their pursuers came up. The archers already had begun to shoot at us, when the boat touched the bank. Hurriedly our remaining soldiers rushed on board, leaving the commander till last. He standing still until all were in safety was about

---

[1] This (to the end) must be in *Oratio Obliqua.*

F

to follow, when he was struck by a spear thrown from a distance. His men however seized him, dragged him into the boat, and rowing vigorously escaped to the other side.

LV.

From that moment the position of the Spaniards became hopeless. The boats no longer ventured to approach them, and they were forced to abandon their vessels and leave their companions to the mercy of the enemy. A few only escaped, others sought shelter on land during the night, but when day broke they were easily captured by the English.

LVI.

The palace stood on an eminence raised about thirty yards above the surface of the lake. It was divided into many courts built with greater or less magnificence, since some were designed for the rich, others for the poor. The roof rested on massive arches of stone, joined by a cement which grew harder by time. Thus the building stood from year to year without any damage from the ravages of rain and wind, and needing no repair.

LVII.

This bridge of boats is so narrow that two carriages cannot pass over abreast. For this reason if two carriages happen to come up on opposite sides of the river at the same time, they both rush violently down the steep bank to the bridge, each trying to get on the roadway first. The muddy yellow stream flows very fast under the boats, and keeps the cables well stretched. It bears on its surface all sorts of nastiness, but the Hindoos tell us that nothing can pollute the waters of the holy Ganges. By the bank close to the bridge stands a man washing clothes; within a few feet of him we see the corpse of a native woman on which are seated some crows and a vulture. Higher up the stream, in cleaner water, elephants are enjoying their morning bath.

LVIII.

The emperor and his nobles stood on the shore awaiting the result of this adventure. They saw the ships move forward in a large crescent form, but they could not discern me, as I was up to my breast in water. When I advanced into the middle of the channel the water reached my neck. The emperor then feared that I was drowned, and that the enemy's fleet was approaching in a hostile manner. I however soon put an end to his fears, for the channel growing shallower at every step, I came in a short time within hearing; then holding up the rope with which I was drawing the fleet I cried out, ' Long live the Emperor of Lilliput ! '

LIX.

Then Nicias, seeing the army in despair, went along the ranks encouraging the soldiers as best he could under the circumstances. ' Soldiers of Athens,' he exclaimed, ' we ought still to hope; before now men have come safe out of worse perils than these ; and you ought not to blame yourselves overmuch either for your disasters or for your present undeserved miseries. My own hope of the future is strong. The enemy seem to have had sufficient good-fortune already, and if we came on this expedition under the jealousy of any god, we have been amply punished. It is therefore only right that we should now hope to deserve the pity of the gods rather than their resentment. Consider also that there is no city in Sicily that could resist your assault or dislodge you if settled anywhere. As to the march you must yourselves take good heed that it be safe and orderly : speed also is requisite throughout your journey, alike by night and day. In one word, soldiers, be well assured that you must quit yourselves as brave men, seeing that there is no place near whither you may escape, if you play the coward's part. Consider this also, that the Athenians will now once again raise up the great power of Athens, though it be fallen ; for it is men that constitute a city, not walls or ships that are void of men.'

LX.

Philip now returned from Illyria into Thessaly, and it was on this occasion that the following circumstance took place.

A Macedonian officer, who had received many honours from the king on account of his bravery, was cast by a storm upon the coast, where the owner of a neighbouring estate found him and ordered him to be taken to his house. At this place the officer was attended to for forty days, until his recovery was complete. Apparently grateful he left the house of his benefactor, but he had seen with envious eyes the prosperity of the man, and now begged the king to give him, as a reward for past services, the estate of his preserver. When this shameful request had been granted by Philip, the ungrateful man drove the wretched owner from his property. The man thus robbed went to the king and told him how he had saved the life of the officer, and what had been his reward. Philip after investigation, finding that the man's story was true, restored the estate to its owner, and ordered the treacherous officer to be branded on the forehead ; for hospitality was ever held by the Greeks to be a sacred duty.

LXI.

Philip continued his march from Phōcis to Boeōtia, and encamped his army in the plain of Chaerōnea. The army of the Greeks marched forward to the river Thermōdōn. Ancient oracles had foretold that this river would be the scene of a terrible disaster to Greece. On the morning of the fatal day which was to decide the destiny of Greece, the armies before sunrise placed themselves in order of battle. The king stood on the right wing, opposite him the Athenians. Alexander, then but nineteen years old, commanded the left, over against the Thebans. Auxiliaries occupied the centre of each army. The Athenians, with matchless valour, and above all the love of liberty, rushed on Philip's phalanx. The right wing and centre of the Macedonian army soon gave way. But while the Athenians were pursuing these, the Thebans were overpowered by Alexander, and their confusion was completed by the Thessalian cavalry whom Alexander sent into the midst of them. Philip meanwhile occupied a rising-ground that was near, and advancing from this position he attacked the ranks of the Athenians who stormed against the phalanx without any order. More than a thousand died by the Macedonian spears, two thousand were taken prisoners, and the rest saved themselves by flight. Orders were immediately given by the king to stop the carnage, seeing that he now looked upon the Greeks as his own subjects.

LXII.

Xerxes had already begun to despair as to the possibility of forcing the pass, when an inhabitant of the district, by name Ephialtes, offered himself to conduct the Persians by a path over the mountains to the rear of the Greeks. Leōnidas was soon informed by a deserter of the march of the Persians, and presently the scouts running down from the heights announced to him that the pass was surrounded. Leonidas now urged the allies to withdraw and reserve themselves for the defence of their country, but declared that he and his three hundred Spartans would not abandon their post. All therefore departed except the Thespians and Thebans, and on the following night the small band that was left attacked the Persian camp. They overpowered the guards, and forced their way even into the tent of the king, who had already made his escape. Upon this they spread themselves among the tents which stood near, and made a terrible slaughter. At last, when the day dawned, the Persians, perceiving the small number of their antagonists, showered their arrows upon the conquerors. Leonidas fell fighting valiantly, and a terrible conflict arose for his body. At last the Spartans rescued it by their valour, and succeeded in carrying it away with them. Once more they drew up in array, but soon all fell under the arrows of the Persians.

LXIII.

When Mardonius received news of the departure of the Greeks, in order to complete his victory he led his Persians at full speed across the Asōpus in pursuit of the Lacedaemonians and Tegeans. The rest, seeing the Persians advancing, threw themselves with a wild shout and without order upon the Lacedaemonians, who were awaiting the result of their sacrifices. As long as the victims were unpropitious, they sustained the attack of the enemy: but when after some time the signs became favourable, they at once set themselves in array and advanced against the Persians. Mardonius distinguished himself by his bravery, and as long as he was at the head of his army the Persians did not give way; but after he had fallen the courage of his people sank, and they fled in disorder to their camp. After a long and obstinate contest the Greeks broke through the fortifications, and rushed into the camp of the barbarians. The wooden wall and towers, which the Persians had constructed for their defence, now proved their destruction. It is said that out of three hundred thousand men scarcely a hundredth part escaped the sword of the Greeks. Eleven days after the battle the conquerors marched to Thebes and demanded the surrender of the principal citizens: these were accordingly given up to avert the destruction of their city.

LXIV.

After they had finished talking, Sōcrates went into an adjoining chamber to bathe himself, Crito following him, while we remained conversing together about what we had just heard. It seemed to us as if we had lost a father, and were doomed to pass the rest of our lives as orphans. Presently Socrates returned to us, and it was now nearly sunset, for he had spent some time with Crito inside. When the officer of the Eleven came and told him that the hour of his death was now near at hand, he said, 'Crito, we must now do as this man tells us: therefore if the poison be ready, let it be brought; if not, let the man prepare (τρίβω) some.' Crito in his turn implored Socrates to make no haste, as there was yet time; but he only replied, 'Do as I desire you.' Upon this Crito made a sign to the servant standing near, and he went out to summon the man who was to administer the poison; he presently appeared holding the cup in his hand. Then said Socrates to him, 'You, my friend, are experienced in these matters; tell me what I must do.'

'Nothing,' answered the man, 'except walk about until you feel a heaviness in your legs, and then lie down; the poison will act of itself:' and with that he held out the cup to Socrates.

LXV.

Socrates took the cup very cheerfully, and looking earnestly at the man asked him if he might pour out any portion of the contents as a libation to the gods. The man replied, 'We prepare only just so much as we think sufficient.' Till this moment we had been able to restrain our sorrow; but now that we saw Socrates drinking, and that he had presently finished the draught, we could no longer forbear, and our tears flowed fast. Socrates alone remained calm, and bade us cease our lamentations and be no more faint-hearted. We then felt ashamed and left off weeping. Socrates walked about for awhile, and then lay down as he had been directed. The man presently touched his feet and legs, and asked if he felt anything. 'No,' replied Socrates: then touching himself he said that as soon as the poison reached his heart he would expire. He then uncovered himself and spoke these his last words: 'Crito, we owe a cock to Asclēpius; do not neglect to pay it.' Besides this he said no more, but after a short interval he made a movement, and his eyes remained fixed. When Crito saw this he closed his mouth and his eyes. Such was the end of Socrates, a man of all whom we have known without doubt the best, and withal the most just and wise.

APPENDIX.

THE following sentences, composed chiefly to illustrate abstract and metaphorical phrases, will require *recasting in form*, according to Greek usage, before translation. For rules and examples the student is referred to Sidgwick's *Greek Prose Composition*, 'Notes on Idiom,' pp. 50–65, and on 'Metaphors,' pp. 93–95.

The Vocabulary will not be of any use here.

1. Amid a general silence Alcibiades rose and spoke as follows.

2. In such cases self-preservation is an obvious duty.

3. The project is surrounded by difficulties, that seem for the present insuperable.

4. For a long while the army was kept in ignorance of its destination.

5. What you have just said is a serious imputation upon my honesty.

6. The failure of this enterprise was a blow to all his expectations.

7. There is no practical difference between these two courses of action.

8. Let us not sacrifice the welfare of the community to the caprice of individuals.

9. Their paucity of numbers was more than counter-balanced by their courage and resolution.

10. The Athenians refused to accept any overtures of peace from the Lacedaemonians.

11. He expressed his annoyance, mingled with surprise, at the ill-success of his darling project.

12. Let us take every precaution to prevent the bare suspicion of injustice in this matter.

13. Zēno the philosopher, while at the court of Phalaris, advised his abdication.

14. The tyrant, suspecting Zeno of designs upon his crown, ordered him to the torture.

15. But Zeno refused to submit, regarding it as an outrage upon justice and humanity.

16. He upbraided the citizens with cowardice in allowing the execution of such a decree, and incited them to resistance.

17. Exasperated at the tyrant's cruelty they flew to arms, overpowered the guards and stoned Phalaris to death.

18. After the expulsion of the Thirty Tyrants democracy was re-established at Athens.

19. Agathocles, accused of theft, was caught with the money concealed about his person.

20. At this crisis the Lesbians determined to make a bold stroke for their liberty.

21. After a protracted debate the motion was carried unanimously.

22. He then assumed a tone of authority, that left no doubt as to his pretensions.

23. The qualifications of Nicias as a general have been overrated by successive historians.

24. It was urged that such concessions on the part of the Athenians would be a compromise of their dignity.

25. I shall have much pleasure in making the acquaintance of so excellent a man as your brother.

26. I cannot see the necessity of such a course of action as you are now prescribing.

27. Experience teaches us that appearances are often most deceptive.

28. He has been reduced from a state of affluence to one of absolute penury.

29. His fortitude upon this trying occasion demands our respect and admiration.

30. Upon these tidings a deep and ominous silence prevailed throughout the assembly.

31. The object of Callicrates in this transaction is utterly incomprehensible.

32. I will not submit to anyone's interference in this important matter.

33. Though there is no apparent danger, we must provide for every contingency, however remote.

34. After a severe struggle the Arcadians at length came off victorious in the field.

35. During this period of anarchy every man did what was right in his own eyes.

36. By courage and perseverance alone we can hope to win the day.

37. His instructions were confined to the delivery of the message without note or comment.

38. This boy's industry has won the approbation of all his masters.

39. The partisans of Callicrates formed a combination for the overthrow of the government.

40. On my arrival I found to my surprise and regret that you had left no message for me.

41. I consider this an act of ill-timed and misplaced confidence on the part of Hippias.

42. I have no time to give the details of the story, but the leading facts are as follows.

43. If you persist in this course, you will become a laughing-stock to your neighbours.

44. You will never argue me into compliance upon such considerations as these.

45. The obscurity of his position has been a bar to the due recognition of his services to the state.

46. From this time forward Xenicles used the language of opposition and revolt.

47. The deplorable condition of the retreating army no words can describe.

48. The Thebans, confident of victory, met with an unexpected reverse.

49. On this subject I cannot speak with certainty; my impression is that the magistrates are greatly to blame.

50. Discretion has been truly said to be the better part of valour.

51. The administration was in the hands of a few individuals, who formed the dominant party in the state.

52. At such a crisis as the present, a hasty decision may bring about an irreparable calamity.

53. Retribution often treads closely upon the heels of crime.

54. Consideration for the feelings of others is a necessary ingredient in a noble nature.

55. The dominion of Alexander over the Persians was secured by his victory at Arbēla (*n. pl.*).

56. Certain philosophers have held that suicide is not only defensible, but even in some cases meritorious.

57. By his inflammatory harangues he lighted the torch of sedition and kindled the flames of civil war.

58. The consequences of such a policy are easy to foresee but difficult to exaggerate.

59. Even his most earnest admirers admit some serious defects in his character.

60. Energy and promptitude, patience and self-control are essential qualities in a commander.

VOCABULARY.

IF the word required is not to be found, look out some common synonym; thus for *foe* see *enemy*, for *town* see *city*, &c. In many instances however direct reference is given; as *abandon = leave, assail = attack,* &c.

When a verb compounded with a preposition is printed thus—(κατ)αγγέλλω, (ἀπ)οίχομαι, &c., either the simple or the compound form may be used at discretion.

For personal, possessive, and some other common pronouns, also for prepositions with their respective cases, refer to the Grammar.

A.

abandon = *leave, desert.*

able, am, δύναμαι, also οἷός τέ εἰμι, and ἔχω.

about, am (to do), μέλλω, often rendered by the fut. of a verb, or by ὡς with fut. part. *I am about* (a thing) = *am engaged in,* or *am doing,* πράσσω, ποιέω.

abroad, am or go, ἀποδημέω.

absent, am, ἄπειμι.

abstain from, ἀπέχομαι (gen.).

accept, δέχομαι, λαμβάνω.

accident, τύχη.

accompany, συνέρχομαι, ὁμιλέω (dat.).

accord, of one's own, ἑκών. See willingly.

accordingly. See under so, thus.

account, on one's, ἕνεκα (gen.), διά (acc.).

accuse, αἰτιάομαι, κατηγορέω (gen.).

accustom, ἐθίζω: *am accustomed,* εἴωθα.

acknowledge, ὁμολογέω (often in middle voice).

acquit, ἀπολύω.

act, ποιέω, πράττω: *act impiously, unjustly,* &c., see under corresponding adverbs.

action, πρᾶγμα (τό): *do a good* or *bad action,* use the corresponding adverbs with ποιέω, &c.

address, (προσ)αγορεύω.

admiral, ναύαρχος.

admire, θαυμάζω.

admit, (1) εἰσδέχομαι, εἰσάγομαι, also εἰσιέναι, ἐάω. (2) = *acknowledge.*

adorn, κοσμέω.

adornment, κόσμος.

advance, προβαίνω, προχωρέω.

advice, βουλή, συμβουλία.

advise, συμβουλεύω, παραινέω (dat.).

affair, πρᾶγμα: *the affairs of* state, &c., τὰ τῆς πόλεως, &c.

afraid, am = *fear.*

after, (1) preposition. (2) conjunction, ἐπεί, ἐπειδή. (3) adverb = *afterwards.*

afternoon, δείλη.

afterwards, ἔπειτα, μετὰ ταῦτα, ὕστερον.

again, αὖ, αὖθις, πάλιν.

age(= time of life), ἡλικία : *a man of (my, your, &c.) age,* τηλικοῦτος.

ago. See long ago.

agree, ὁμολογέω, συγχωρέω, συντίθεμαι. *It is agreed* (to do, &c.), δοκεῖ.

agreeable = *pleasant.*

alarmed, ἔμφοβος. See fear.

Alexander, Ἀλέξανδρος.

alive, am, ζάω.

allow, (1) ἐάω, also περιοράω. (2) = *acknowledge.*

allowed, am, ἔξεστί μοι.

ally, σύμμαχος.

almost = *nearly.*

alone, μόνος (sometimes use αὐτός).

already, ἤδη.

also, καί.

altar, βῶμος, ἐσχάρα.

although, καίπερ (with part.), εἰ καί.

always, ἀεί.

am in, ἔνειμι : *am with,* σύνειμι.

ambassador, πρέσβυς (in plural), πρεσβευτής.

amount of, (such an) = (*so*) *much.*

amply, ἀποχρώντως.

anchor, ἀγκύρα, (verb) ὁρμέω.

ancient, παλαιός, ἀρχαῖος.

anger, χόλος, ὀργή, (of gods) μῆνις (ἡ).

angry, am, ὀργίζομαι, ἀγανακτέω : *get angry,* χαλεπαίνω.

animal, ζῶον.

announce, (κατ)αγγέλλω.

another, ἄλλος, (of two) ἕτερος : *another sort of,* ἀλλοῖος.

answer, ἀποκρίνομαι : *answer a signal,* ἀντισημαίνω.

Antipho, Ἀντιφῶν (-ῶντος).

any, anyone, τις : *not any,* οὐδείς (μηδείς).

anywhere, που, (of motion) ποι.

ape, πίθηκος.

appear, (1) = *seem.* (2) *am visible, come in sight,* φαίνομαι, often παραγίγνομαι, also πάρειμι.

applaud, ἐπαινέω, ἐπιθορυβέω.

appointed = *agreed upon.*

approach, προσέρχομαι, προσχωρέω.

approve, ἐπαινέω, συναινέω.

arch, ἁψίς (-ῖδος), ἡ.

archer, τοξότης.

arise, (1) = *rise.* (2) = *become.*

arm, (verb) ὁπλίζω : *armed* (for battle) ὡπλισμένος.

arms, ὅπλα.

army, στράτευμα, στρατός, στρατιά.

array, (noun) τάξις (ἡ), (verb) τάσσω.

arrive, ἀφικνέομαι, πάρειμι, also ἥκω.

arrow, οἰστός, τόξευμα.

art, τέχνη.

as, (1) of manner, ὡς. (2) of time, ὡς, ὅτε (often rendered by a participle). (3) causal = *since,* ἐπεί.

as if, ὥσπερ, ὡς with part.

ascend, ἐπιβαίνω (usually followed by ἐπί with accusative).

ashamed, am, αἰσχύνομαι.

ask, (1) a question, ἔρομαι, ἐρωτάω. (2) *ask for* a thing, αἰτέω, δέομαι (gen.).

asleep, am. See sleep.

ass, ὄνος.

assail = *attack.*

assemble, (1) trans. συλλέγω, συγκαλέω. (2) intrans. συνέρχομαι, or passive of συλλέγω.

assign, (δια)νέμω.

associate with, (συν)ομιλέω.

Assyrian, Ἀσσύριος.

astonished, am, θαυμάζω, ἐκπλήσσομαι.

at all. See not at all.

Athenian, Ἀθηναῖος.

Athens, Ἀθῆναι (αἱ).

attack, (verb) ἐπιτίθεμαι, προσ-

βάλλω, ἐπέρχομαι, (noun) προσβολή.
attempt, πειράομαι, ἐπιχειρέω.
auxiliaries, ἐπίκουροι.
avenge oneself on, ἀμύνομαι, (acc.).
avert, ἀποτρέπω.
aware, am = know.
away, am, ἄπειμι : go away, see under go.
awhile. See while.
axe, πέλεκυς (ὁ).

B.

bad, κακός, πονηρός.
bag, θύλακος.
banish, ἐξελαύνω : am banished, ἐκπίπτω, also φεύγω.
bank (of river), ὄχθη : on the banks of, use simply ἐπί (with name of river).
banquet, δεῖπνον, συμπόσιον.
bar, μοχλός.
barbarian, βάρβαρος.
barley, κριθή (in plural).
bathe, λούομαι.
battle, μάχη.
bean, κύαμος.
bear (in all senses), φέρω. See also endure, suffer.
beast, θήρ, θηρίον.
beat, κόπτω, τύπτω (in some tenses). See also strike.
beat off, ἀποκρούω.
beautiful, καλός.
beauty, κάλλος (τό).
because, ὅτι.
become, (1) γίγνομαι. (2) = suit, πρέπω : it becomes (one) πρέπει, προσήκει.
become of (anyone), γενέσθαι (with dat. of person).
bed, κοίτη, κλίνη : go to bed, κοιμάομαι, κατακεῖμαι.
before, (1) adv. πρότερον. (2) conj. πρίν, πρὶν ἤ. (3) prep. πρό,

ἀντί : (= in presence of) ἐναντίον.
beforehand, am, φθάνω with part., or part. of φθάνω with verb.
beg = ask, entreat.
begin, ἄρχομαι with gen. ; begin (to do), often rendered by imperf.
behave oneself (as), παρέχω ἐμαυτόν, often γίγνομαι.
behave among (men), ὁμιλέω (dat.).
behind, ὄπισθε(ν), ὀπίσω.
behold, θεωρέω, βλέπω, ὁράω.
believe, πιστεύω, πείθομαι (dat.).
belong to, προσήκειν (dat.); belonging to, πρός with acc., or use the possessive genitive.
below, κάτω, but often rendered by a compound with ὑπό. See lie below.
benefactor, εὐεργέτης, or use part. of verb.
benefit (verb) ὠφελέω, εὖ ποιέω, (noun) ὄφελος (τό), εὐεργεσία, ἀγαθόν.
besiege, πολιορκέω.
bestow, δίδωμι, ἐπιδίδωμι, also τίθημι.
betray, προδίδωμι.
between, μεταξύ, ἐν μέσῳ (gen.).
beware, φυλάσσομαι : beware lest, &c., ὅρα μή (with subj.), or ὅπως (with fut. ind.).
beyond, ὑπέρ, πέραν (gen.).
bezel (of a ring), σφενδόνη.
bid, κελεύω : bid farewell, χαίρειν λέγω.
bird, ὄρνις (ἡ).
birth, γένος (τό).
bite, δάκνω.
bitterly (weep, &c.) = much, greatly.
black, μέλας.
blame, μέμφομαι, αἰτιάομαι.
blanket, σισύρα.
blest, εὐδαίμων, μακάριος.
blind, τυφλός.
blood, αἷμα (τό).

boar, ὗς.

board, go on, εἰσβαίνω (with or without εἰς) ναῦν : *put on board*, ἀναβιβάζομαι (ἐπί).

boat, πλοῖον.

body, σῶμα.

Boeotian, Βοιωτός.

bonds, δεσμὰ (τά).

bone, ὀστέον.

book, βιβλίον.

bore (out), (ἐκ)τρυπάω.

borrow, χράομαι in 1 aor. ; *borrow money*, δανείζομαι.

both, (adj.) ἄμφω, ἀμφότεροι.

both . . . and, (conj.) καὶ . . . καί, τε . . . καί.

bottom (of river or lake), βάθη (τά).

boy, παῖς : *little boy*, παίδιον.

branch, κλάδος, ὄζος.

brand, (verb) στίζω.

brass, χαλκός : (*made*) *of brass*, *brazen*, χαλκέος.

brave, ἀγαθός, ἀνδρεῖος.

bravely, εὖ, κρατερῶς (καρτερῶς).

bread, ἄρτος.

breadth, εὖρος (τό).

break, κατάγνυμι, ῥήγνυμι, (a treaty) λύω : *break down* (a bridge), (κατα)λύω : *break in pieces*, διακλάω.

break of day. See day.

breast, στῆθος (τό).

brick, πλίνθος.

bridge, γέφυρα.

bright, λαμπρός.

bring, φέρω, ἄγω : *bring back*, κατάγω : *bring in*, εἰσφέρω : *bring round*, περιάγω : *bring upon*, ἐπάγω : *bring to pass*, ἀποτελέω : *bring word*, καταγγέλλω.

broad, εὐρύς.

brother, ἀδελφός.

build, οἰκοδομέω, ποιέομαι.

builder, οἰκοδόμος.

building, οἰκοδομή.

bull, ταῦρος.

bundle, δεσμή.

burden, φόρτιον.

burn, (trans.) καίω, (intrans.) αἴθομαι.

burrow, καταδύομαι.

burst, (κατα)ρρήγνυμι.

business, it is (anyone's), use δεῖ or χρή.

busy, am, ἀσχολέομαι, ἄσχολός εἰμι.

but, ἀλλά, δέ (commonly with μέν in preceding clause).

buy, ὠνέομαι, (πρίασθαι), ἀγοράζω.

C.

cable, κάλως (-ω).

calf, μόσχος.

call, καλέω : *call for*, (ἐπι)καλέω : *call by name*, ὀνομάζω.

calm, ἥσυχος.

camel, κάμηλος.

camp, στρατόπεδον.

captain, (military) λοχαγός, (naval) ναύκληρος.

captive, δεσμώτης, δεδεμένος, (in war) αἰχμάλωτος.

capture, αἱρέω, in passive ἁλίσκομαι.

care, care for, μέλει (μοι, &c.).

care, take. See beware.

Carian, Κάρ, (adj.) Καρικός.

carnage, φόνος, σφαγή.

carpenter, τέκτων, ξυλουργός.

carriage, ἅρμα (τό).

carry, φέρω, κομίζω : *carry away*, ἀποφέρω, ἐκκομίζω : *carry out*, (design)=*effect*, *perform*.

case, πρᾶγμα, also=*fortune* ; *to be the case*, οὕτως ἔχειν.

cat, αἴλουρος.

catch, αἱρέω, λαμβάνω, συλλαμβάνω : *catch hold of*, κρατέω, λαμβάνομαι (gen.).

cattle, πρόβατα (τά).

cause, (verb) ποιέω, also παρέχω : (noun) αἰτία : *the cause of*, &c., τὰ τῶν, &c.

cautious, εὐλαβής: *am cautious,* εὐλαβέομαι. See also beware.

cavalry, ἱππεῖς (οἱ).

cease, παύομαι.

cement, τέλμα (τό).

certain, σαφής: *am certain,* εὖ or σαφῶς οἶδα, πιστεύω: *a certain one,* τις.

certainly, ἀληθῶς, σαφῶς, φανερῶς, also δή.

chamber, οἴκημα (τό).

chance, τύχη.

charge, (1) = *enjoin,* ἐφίεμαι, κελεύω. (2) = *accuse,* αἰτιάομαι. (3) *in battle,* ἐλαύνω (εἰς), προσιππεύω.

charge of, take, ἐπιμελέομαι (gen.).

chariot, ἅρμα (τό).

chase = *pursue.*

chasm, χάσμα (τό).

cheer, have good, εὐωχέομαι.

cheerful, ἵλεως, ἱλαρός.

cheese, τυρός.

chest, κίστη, θήκη.

chicken, νεοσσός.

chief, chieftain, ἄρχων.

child, παῖς, παιδίον, τέκνον.

choose, αἱρέομαι: *choose* (to do, &c.) = *wish.*

chosen, ἐπίλεκτος, αἱρετός.

circumstance, πρᾶγμα: *the circumstances,* τὰ παρόντα.

citadel, ἀκρόπολις (ἡ).

citizen, πολίτης.

city, πόλις, ἄστυ (τό).

claim, ἀξιόω.

clean, καθαρός.

Cleander, Κλέανδρος.

clear (1) = *bright.* (2) = *evident.*

clearly = *evidently.*

clever, σοφός, δεινός.

cleverly, σοφῶς.

climb up = *ascend, go up.*

cloak, ἱμάτιον.

close = *shut; close* (eyes), συλλαμβάνω.

close quarters (to), εἰς χεῖρας, ὁμόσε, or = *near.*

clothes, ἱμάτια (τά), ἐσθής (ἡ), (in sing.).

cloud, νεφέλη.

coast, ἀκτή : *on the coast,* ἐπιθαλάσσιος, often ἐπὶ τῇ θαλάσσῃ, also οἱ κάτω.

coast along, παραπλέω.

cock, ἀλεκτρύων (-ονος).

cold, (adj.) ψυχρός: (noun) ψῦχος (τό) : *am cold,* ῥιγόω.

colt, πῶλος.

combustible, καυσιμός.

come, ἔρχομαι: *am come,* ἥκω, πάρειμι: *come down,* καταβαίνω: *come from* = *arrive: come in* or *into,* εἰσέρχομαι: *come on,* (1) προβαίνω. (2) = *ensue,* γίγνομαι, ἐπιγίγνομαι: *come to,* προσέρχομαι: *come up,* προσέρχομαι, ἀφικνέομαι: *come upon,* ἐπέρχομαι, ἐπιτίθεμαι.

command, (noun) ἀρχή : (verb) ἄρχω, στρατηγέω: = *bid,* κελεύω.

commander, ἄρχων, (of an army) στρατηγός, (of ships) ναύαρχος.

commend = *praise.*

commit crimes, κακῶς ποιέω, ἀδικέω.

common, κοινός.

companion, ἑταῖρος.

company, usually οἱ παρόντες.

company, keep, ὁμιλέω.

compel, ἀναγκάζω, βιάζομαι.

complain, ἀγανακτέω, δεινὸν ποιέομαι.

conceal, (κατα)κρύπτω.

concerns, it, προσήκει (dat.) ; *it is no concern of,* οὐδὲν διαφέρει (dat.), or οὐδὲν πρός (acc.).

condemn, κατακρίνω.

condition, on, ἐφ' ᾧ, ἐφ' ᾧτε: *on these conditions,* ἐπὶ τούτοις.

conduct (one's), usually rendered by passive part. of πράσσω or ποιέω.

confess, ὁμολογέω.

confines, ὅρια (τά).
conflict = *battle*.
congratulate, εὐδαιμονίζω, μακαρίζω.
conjecture, εἰκάζω.
conjure (= *beseech*), ἱκετεύω.
conquer, νικάω, in passive also ἡσσάομαι.
conqueror, use part. of νικάω.
consider, (1) νομίζω, ἡγέομαι. (2) ἐνθυμέομαι. (3) σκοπέω.
consist in, συνέχεσθαι.
conspire against, ἐπιβουλεύω.
consternation, ἔκπληξις (ἡ).
consult, (trans.) ἀνακοινόω, (intrans.) (συμ)βουλεύομαι.
contend, ἀγωνίζομαι. See also fight.
contented, am, ἀρκεῖ (μοι).
continually, ἀεί.
continue = *remain*; *continue* (doing, &c.), διατελέω, or by imperf.
contrary, ἐναντίος, (of winds) also σκαιός.
contrive, μηχανάομαι, διαπράσσομαι.
convey, κομίζω, φέρω.
copper, χαλκός.
Corcyra, Κέρκυρα.
Corcyraean, Κερκυραῖος.
Corinth, Κόρινθος (ἡ).
corn, σῖτος.
corpse, νεκρός.
cottage, ἔπαυλις (ἡ).
council, βουλή : *hold a council*, συμβουλεύομαι.
country, γῆ, χώρα: *native country*, πατρίς: *of what country*, ποδαπός: *up the country*, ἄνω.
courage, θάρσος (τό), ἀρετή, εὐψυχία.
course, δρόμος, or = *way*, (of a ship) πλόος.
course, of (in answers), πάνυ γε, πῶς γὰρ οὔ.
court, αὐλή, βασίλειον : *courts* (separate), αὐλαί.

coward, δειλός : *am a coward*, ἀποδειλιάω, μαλακίζομαι.
cowardice, δειλία.
crescent-formed, μηνοειδής.
crime, ἀδίκημα, ἁμάρτημα (τό).
cross (river, &c.), διαβαίνω.
crow, κορώνη, κόραξ.
crown, (noun) στέφανος : (verb) στεφανόω.
cruel, χαλεπός, ὠμός, ἄγριος.
cry, (1) = *weep*, κλαίω. (2) = *shout*, *cry out*, (ἀνα)βοάω.
cup, κύλιξ (ἡ), ποτήριον.
custom, ἔθος (τό) : *according to custom*, κατὰ τὸ εἰωθός.
cut, τέμνω : *cut down* (trees, &c.), κόπτω, ἐκκόπτω : *cut off*, ἀποτέμνω : *cut through*, διακόπτω.

D.

dance, ὀρχέομαι.
danger, κίνδυνος : *am in danger*, κινδυνεύω.
Danube, Ἴστρος.
dare, τολμάω.
Darius, Δαρεῖος.
dark, σκοτεινός.
darkness, σκότος (τό).
daughter, θυγάτηρ.
day, ἡμέρα: *every day*, καθ᾽ ἡμέραν: *next day*, τῇ ὑστεραίᾳ: *the day before*, τῇ προτεραίᾳ: *this same* or *very day*, αὐθήμερον: *to this day* (= *to this time*), εἰς τόδε : *at daybreak* or *dawn*, ἅμα τῇ ἡμέρᾳ.
deal with = *use*.
dear, φίλος.
death, θάνατος : *put to death*, ἀποκτείνω.
deceive, (ἐξ)απατάω.
decide, κρίνω, διακρίνω : *it is decided* or *I decide* (to do, &c.), δοκεῖ μοι, &c.
deem = *think*.
deep, βαθύς : deeply (in phrases like *deeply grieved*, &c.) = *very much*.

defeat, am defeated. See conquer.

defend, ἀμύνω (dat.), also = *help*; *defend oneself*, ἀμύνομαι ‚accus.); *defend one's ground*, κατὰ χώραν μένω.

degrees, by, κατὰ μικρόν.

deity, θεός, τὸ θεῖον.

delay, (verb) χρονίζω, μέλλω: (noun) τριβή, μέλλησις.

deliver, (1) ἀποδίδωμι. (2) = *save, set free.*

demand, (ἀπ)αιτέω, ἀξιόω.

deny, ἀρνέομαι, also οὔ φημι.

depart, οἴχομαι, ἀπέρχομαι.

depends on, (you, &c.), ἐν σοί, &c., ἐστί.

deposit = *put, place (in).*

deprive, ἀποστερέω.

désert, *deserted*, ἔρημος.

desért, ἀπολείπω.

deserter, αὐτόμολος.

deserve, ἄξιός εἰμι (gen.).

design, (1) = *intend.* (2) = *make, build*, &c.

desire, ἐπιθυμέω (gen.), = *wish* (todo). βούλομαι, θέλω, = *request, bid*, αἰτέω, κελεύω.

despair, am in, ἀθυμέω, ἄθυμός εἰμι.

despise, καταφρονέω (gen.).

destroy, ἀπόλλυμι (of cities, &c.), διαφθείρω, πορθέω (of bridges). See break down.

destruction, ὄλεθρος.

determined, it is, δοκεῖ.

devour, κατεσθίω.

die, θνήσκω, τελευτάω.

differ, διαφέρω: (there) *is a difference*, διαφέρει.

different, διαφέρων, also ἄλλος, ἀλλοῖος.

difficult, χαλεπός.

difficulty, τὸ χαλεπόν: (= *straits*) ἀπορία: *am in difficulties*, ἀπορέω.

dine, δειπνέω.

dining-room, ἀνώγεων (τό).

dinner, δεῖπνον.

direction of, in the. ἐπί (with gen.); *in all directions*, κατὰ πάντα: *in different directions*, ἄλλοι ἄλλη.

directly, εὐθύς, εὐθέως.

disaster, συμφορά.

discern, διακρίνω, also = *see, perceive.*

disciple, μαθητής.

discover, εὑρίσκω, καταλαμβάνω, γιγνώσκω.

discreetly, σωφρόνως, φρονίμως.

disease, νόσος (ἡ).

disgraceful, αἰσχρός.

dislike, μισέω, also οὐ φιλέω.

dislodge, ἐξανίστημι.

disobey, ἀπειθέω.

disperse, διασπείρω.

display, φαίνω, ἐπιδείκνυμι.

distant, am, ἀπέχω : from a distance, πόρρωθεν.

distinguished, διαπρεπής.

distress = *grief*, or ἀπορία: *am in distress*, ἀπορέω, λυπέομαι.

distribute, (δια)νέμω, διαιρέω.

district, χώρα.

disturb, ταράσσω.

dive, καταδύομαι, and 2 aor. of active voice.

divide, μερίζω, διανέμω.

division (of an army), στράτευμα.

do, ποιέω, πράσσω, δράω. The passive is often rendered by γίγνεσθαι: *do with* (anyone or anything), χράομαι (dat.).

doctor, ἰατρός.

dog, κύων.

dolphin, δελφίς (-ῖνος).

dominion, ἀρχή.

door, θύρα.

doubt, (verb) ἀπορέω: (noun) ἀπορία.

doubtful, ἀμφίβολος.

downcast (in mind), δεδουλωμένος.

drag, ἕλκω, ἄγω.

dragon, δράκων (-οντος).

draw = σπάω, also = *drag*.
drink, πίνω: *drink up*, καταπίνω, ἐκπίνω.
drive, ἐλαύνω, ἄγω, also = *banish*.
drown, καταποντίζω.
drunk, am, μεθύω.
due, ἄξιος, (of money) = *owed*.
duty, τὸ δέον, τὰ δέοντα: *it is (my) duty*, χρή, δεῖ, προσήκει (dat.).
dwell, dwell in, οἰκέω, κατοικέω.

E.

each, ἕκαστος: *each other*, ἀλλήλους or ἄλλοι ἄλλους.
eagle, ἀετός.
ear, οὖς (τό).
early, πρωί (πρῶ).
earn, κτάομαι.
earnest, σπουδαῖος, πρόθυμος.
earth, γῆ: *what on earth?* τί ποτε;
earthquake, σεισμός.
easily, ῥᾳδίως.
easy, ῥᾴδιος.
eat, ἐσθίω.
effect, πράσσω, τελέω: *without effecting purpose*, ἄπρακτος.
egg, ᾠόν.
either . . . or, ἤ . . . ἤ.
elders, πρεσβύτεροι: eldest, πρεσβύτατος.
elephant, ἐλέφας.
else (adj.) = *other*, (adv.) ἄλλως.
elsewhere, ἄλλοθι, (of motion) ἄλλοσε.
eminence = *hill*.
employ = *use*.
enact (laws), τίθημι.
encamp, στρατοπεδεύομαι.
encourage, παραθαρσύνω.
end, τέλος (τό), τελευτή, *be at an end* (of a truce), διαλύεσθαι: *put an end to*, παύω.
endure, (1) φέρω, ἀνέχομαι. (2) (δια)μένω. (3) καρτερέω.
enemy (in war), πολέμιος: (private) ἐχθρός.

English, Ἄγγλος.
enmity, ἔχθρα: *incur enmity*, ἀπέχθομαι (dat.).
enough, ἅλις.
enrage, (ἐξ)οργίζω.
enslave, (κατα)δουλόω.
enter, εἰσέρχομαι.
entertain (guests), ξενίζω, δέχομαι.
entreat, αἰτέω, δέομαι (gen.).
envoy = *ambassador*.
envy, (noun) φθόνος: (verb) φθονέω, ζηλόω.
equal, ἴσος.
err, ἁμαρτάνω.
escape, ἀποφεύγω, διαφεύγω: *escape knowledge* or *notice*, λανθάνω with part. or verb with λαθών.
estate, χωρίον.
even, καί: *not even*, οὐδέ.
even, (adj.) ἴσος, ὁμαλός.
evening, ἑσπέρα.
ever, ποτέ, mostly after negatives (οὐ, μή, οὐδείς, &c.).
every, πᾶς (without article); *everybody, everyone*, πᾶς τις, or πάντες: *everywhere*, πανταχοῦ.
evident, δῆλος, φανερός, σαφής.
evidently, φανερῶς, σαφῶς: *I evidently am*, usually φανερός, δῆλός εἰμι, or simply φαίνομαι (ὤν).
examination, ζήτησις, ἐξέτασις (ἡ).
examine, ἐξετάζω.
exceedingly, σφόδρα.
excellent, ἄριστος, βέλτιστος.
excellently, ἄριστα, διαφερόντως.
except, εἰ μή.
exclaim, βοάω, or = *say, speak*.
exercise = *practise*; (of the body) γυμνάζω.
exhort, παραινέω, παρακαλέω.
exile, go into, = *am banished*.
expect, ἐλπίζω, προσδοκάω.
expectation, ἐλπίς (ἡ), προσδοκία, also γνώμη, δόξα.
expedient, συμφέρον: *it is expedient*, συμφέρει.

expedition, στρατεία: *go on expedition*, στρατεύω.
explain, ἐξηγέομαι, δηλόω.
extend, (trans.) τείνω, (intrans.) (παρα)τείνομαι.

F.

fable, μῦθος.
face, πρόσωπον, ὄψις (ἡ).
fail, ἐπιλείπω.
fair, (1) καλός. (2) δίκαιος.
faithful, πιστός.
fall, πίπτω ; *fall down*, καταπίπτω : *fall into*, εἰσπίπτω : *fall upon*, ἐπιπίπτω, ἐμπίπτω, or = *attack*.
false, ψευδής.
falsely, ψευδῶς, or neut. pl. of ψευδής : *speak falsely*, ψεύδομαι.
far, (1) = *much*, πολύ. (2) of distance, πρόσω (πόρρω) : *as far as*, μέχρι (gen.), ὅσον : *so far*, τόσον, τοσοῦτον: *so far from*, . . . *that even* = *not only not* . . . *but even* ; *how far* (distant)? πόσον ;
fare, πράσσω, πάσχω.
farmer, γεωργός.
fast, = *quick*, *quickly*.
fat, παχύς, σιτευτός.
father, πατήρ.
fault, ἁμαρτία, ἁμάρτημα (τό).
favour, χάρις (ἡ), εὔνοια.
favourable, ἵλεως, εὐμενής, (of omens) καλός, χρηστός.
fear, (noun) φόβος : (verb) δέδοικα, φοβέομαι.
feast, ἑστιάομαι.
feather, πτέρον.
fee, μισθός.
feed on, τρέφομαι, ἐσθίω : *feed flocks*, νέμω, νομεύω.
fetch, (1) κομίζω (usually in middle). (2) = *be sold for*, εὑρίσκειν.
few, ὀλίγοι, παῦροι, οὐ πολλοί.
fewer, ἐλάσσων (in plural).
field, ἀγρός, (of battle) μάχη.
fierce, ἄγριος.

fight, (verb) μάχομαι : (noun) = *battle*.
find, εὑρίσκω, ἐντυγχάνω (dat.) ; also = *perceive*. The phrase *finding that*, &c. is often rendered by ἐπεί with the verb.
find fault = *blame*.
fine, καλός.
finger, δάκτυλος.
finish, ἐπιτελέω, περαίνω.
fire, πῦρ: *am on fire*, αἴθομαι : *set fire to*, καίω.
first, πρῶτος, (of two) πρότερος.
fish, ἰχθύς.
fix, πήγνυμι: *be fixed*, often στῆναι.
flee, φεύγω, ἀποφεύγω: *flee for refuge*, καταφεύγω.
fleet, ναυτικόν, also ναῦς (in plural).
flight, φυγή.
flog, μαστιγόω.
flow, ῥέω.
fly, πέτομαι: *fly down*, καταπέτομαι : *fly up*, ἀναπέτομαι.
fog, ὁμίχλη.
follow, ἕπομαι : as follows, ὧδε or ταῦτα (εἶπε).
folly, μωρία.
fond of hunting, φιλόθηρος.
food, σῖτος, σιτία (τά).
fool, foolish, μῶρος, ἀνόητος.
foolishly, ἀνοήτως.
foot, πούς (ὁ).
for, (conj.) γάρ.
forage, (verb) ληΐζομαι, ἐπισιτίζομαι.
forbear, ἀπέχομαι, or use μή : *will you not forebear* (doing), οὐ μή, with fut. ind.
forbid, ἀπειπεῖν, ἀπαγορεύω, also οὐκ ἐάω.
force, (verb) βιάζομαι: (noun) βία.
forces = *army*.
forehead, μέτωπον.
foresee, προοράω.
forest, ὕλη.
forget, ἐπιλανθάνομαι, also οὐ μέμνημαι.

forgive, συγγιγνώσκω (dat.).

form, (noun) μορφή: (verb) = make.

formerly, πάλαι, ποτέ.

forsake, = desert.

fort, fortress, τεῖχος, τείχισμα (τό).

fortify, τειχίζω.

fortune, τύχη: good fortune, εὐτυχία.

four times, τετράκις.

fox, ἀλώπηξ (-εκος) ἡ.

free, (adj.) ἐλεύθερος: (verb) ἐλευθερόω, free oneself, also ἀπαλλάσσομαι.

frequent, (verb) φοιτάω (ἐπί).

fresh, νέος or ἄλλοι.

friend, φίλος.

frighten, φοβέω: frightened, also ἔμφοβος.

frog, βάτραχος.

from among, ἐκ (ἐξ).

fugitive, φυγάς, or part. of φεύγω.

full, πλήρης, μεστός.

funeral pile, πυρά.

furlong. See stade.

further, πρόσω, περαιτέρω.

future, the, τὸ μέλλον : in future, for the future, τὸ λοιπόν, ὕστερον.

G.

gain, (noun) κέρδος (τό): (verb) κερδαίνω, or = get; gain ground, προχωρέω, κρατέω: gain victory, νικάω.

garden, κῆπος.

garland, στέφανος.

garment, ἐσθής (-ῆτος), ἡ.

gate, πύλη.

general, στρατηγός.

get, λαμβάνω, κτάομαι : get along, προβαίνω : get on = fare; get off (punishment), ἀποφεύγω: get up = rise.

gild, χρυσόω.

girl, κόρη, παρθένος.

give, δίδωμι : give away, δωρέομαι, χαρίζομαι: give up = surrender ; give way, εἴκω, παραχωρέω:

give for, (a thing) = buy for (so much), with gen. of price.

glad, am = am pleased, rejoice.

gladly, ἡδέως, ἀσμένως.

glorious, κλεινός, ἔνδοξος.

gnat, κώνωψ (-ωπος).

go, εἶμι, βαίνω: go about, περιέρχομαι: go away, ἀπέρχομαι, (ἀπ)οίχομαι : go back, ἀνέρχομαι: ἀναχωρέω : go in or into = enter; go out, ἐξέρχομαι : go through, διέρχομαι : go up, ἀνέρχομαι, ἀναβαίνω : go on, (of events), γίγνομαι, προχωρέω.

god, θεός.

gold, χρυσός.

good, ἀγαθός, χρηστός: be good for (anyone), ὠφελεῖν: do good to, εὖ ποιέω, ὠφελέω.

goods, χρήματα.

good-fortune, εὐτυχία.

goodwill, εὔνοια.

goose, χήν.

governor, ὕπαρχος.

graciously, χαριέντως, εὐμενῶς.

grant, δίδωμι, παρέχω, (a favour) χαρίζομαι.

grass, χόρτος.

grateful, am, χάριν ἔχω, χάριν οἶδα.

gratification = pleasure.

gratify = please.

gratitude, χάρις: get gratitude, χάριν λαμβάνω or κατατίθεμαι.

great, μέγας, how great? πόσος; (rel.) ὅσος: so great, τόσος, τοσοῦτος.

greatly, πολύ, σφόδρα.

Greece, Ἑλλάς (ἡ).

Greek, Ἕλλην, speak Greek, ἑλληνίζω.

grief, λύπη, ἄλγος (τό).

grieve, (trans.) λυπέω, (intrans.) λυπέομαι, ἄχθομαι.

ground, (1) γῆ, πέδον, χώρα. (2) = cause ; on the ground, χαμαί : gain ground. See gain.

grudge, (noun and verb) = envy.

guard, (noun) φύλαξ : (verb) φυλάσσω.

guide, (noun) ἡγεμών : (verb) ἡγέομαι (dat.).

guilty, αἴτιος (gen.).

H.

hair, θρίξ (ἡ), in plural.

half, ἡμισύς.

hand, χείρ (ἡ).

Hannibal, 'Αννίβας (-αντος).

happen, (1) = chance (to be), τυγχάνω. (2) = occur, γίγνομαι : happen to (anyone), συμβαίνω (dat.).

happy, εὐδαίμων : think happy, μακαρίζω.

harbour, λιμήν (ὁ).

hard, (1) σκληρύς, (= solid) στερεός (στερρός). (2) = difficult.

harden, στερεύω.

hardships, χαλεπά, κακά.

hare, λαγώς (-ῶ).

harm, (verb) βλάπτω, κακῶς ποιέω: come to harm = suffer.

harmless, ἀβλαβής, ἀσινής : (of character), ἄκακος.

haste, σπουδή : in haste, σπουδῇ, διὰ σπουδῆς, or use part. of verb.

hasten, σπεύδω, ἐπείγομαι.

hate, μισέω.

haunt, ἔρχομαι ἐπί (accus.).

have, ἔχω, or use ἐστί (μοι, &c.); have to (do, &c.). See must.

head, κεφαλή.

hear, ἀκούω: within hearing, εἰς ἐπήκοον.

hearsay, ἀκοή, or use part. of verb.

heaven, οὐρανός, or use οἱ θεοί.

heavy, βαρύς: heavy-armed, ὁπλίτης.

height. ὕψος (τό): heights, ἄκρα (τά).

Hellespont, 'Ελλήσποντος.

helmet, κράνος (τό).

help, (verb) ὠφελέω, (in war) βοηθέω: (noun) ὠφελία, βοήθεια.

hen, ὄρνις.

hence, ἐντεῦθεν, ἐνθένδε.

herald, κῆρυξ.

herd, ἀγέλη.

herdsman, βουκόλος.

here, ἐνταῦθα, ἐνθάδε : am here, πάρειμι : here is, use ὅδε.

hereupon, ἐνταῦθα, μετὰ ταῦτα.

hesitate, ὀκνέω.

hide, κρύπτω, καλύπτω.

high, ὑψηλύς : higher parts (of town), τὰ μετέωρα.

hill, λόφος.

hinder, κωλύω, also οὐκ ἐάω.

hither, δεῦρο, ἐνθάδε.

hold, ἔχω, κατέχω: hold up, ἀνέχω, (of hands), ἀνατείνω : take hold of, λαμβάνω (in middle), κρατέω (gen.): hold a meeting, σύλλογον ποιέομαι : hold out, (trans.) ἀνατείνω, ὀρέγω, (intrans.) = endure, (δια)καρτερέω.

hollow, κοῖλος.

holy, ἱερός, ἅγιος.

home, οἶκος: at home, οἴκοι : home-(wards), οἴκαδε.

Homer, "Ομηρος.

honey, μέλι (-τος), τό.

honour, (noun) τιμή : (verb) τιμάω.

hope, (noun) ἐλπίς (ἡ) : (verb) ἐλπίζω.

hopeless, ἀνέλπιστος.

horn, κέρας (τό).

horse, ἵππος.

horseman, ἱππεύς.

hospitality, ξενία.

hostile, πολέμιος, πολεμικός : in hostile manner, πολεμίως, or by ὡς with fut. part. of verb attack.

house, οἶκος, οἰκία.

how? πῶς; (indirect) ὅπως: how great? how much? (see great); how many? πόσοι; (rel.) ὅσοι, (ὁπόσοι).

however, ὅμως, also δέ, μέντοι.

hungry, am, πεινάω.

hunt, θηράω, διώκω (θῆρας).

hurl = throw.

hurriedly. See haste.

hurt, (verb) βλάπτω, ἀδικέω:(noun) βλαβή.

I.

idle, ἀργός: *am idle*, ῥᾳθυμέω.
if, εἰ (with ind. and opt.) ; ἐάν (with subj.).
ignorant, ἀμαθής: *am ignorant* (of), ἀγνοέω, οὐκ οἶδα.
ill, am, νοσέω.
image, εἰκών (ἡ), ἄγαλμα (τύ).
imagine, ἐνθυμέομαι, or use εἰκάζω.
immediately = *directly*.
impious, ἀσεβής, ἀνύσιος.
impiously, ἀσεβῶς; *act impiously*, ἀσεβέω.
important, it is, μέγα or πολὺ διαφέρει, περὶ πολλοῦ ἐστι.
impossible, ἀδύνατον.
impudence, ἀναίδεια.
Indian, Ἰνδος.
induce, πείθω; *what induces you?* &c., τί παθών or μαθών; &c.
industrious, φιλόπονος, σπουδαῖος.
infect, ἀναπίμπλημι (gen.).
inhabit = *dwell in*.
inhabitants, (of a town) = *citizens*.
injury, injustice, ἀδικία: *commit injustice*, ἀδικέω.
inland, (adv.) ἄνω: (noun) ἡ μεσογεία, τὰ μεσόγεια.
inside, ἔνδον, ἔσω.
instead of, ἀντί (gen.).
insult, (noun) ὕβρις (ἡ): (verb) ὑβρίζω, λοιδορέομαι.
intemperate, ἀκρατής.
intend (doing), μέλλω, ἐν νῷ ἔχω, or = *wish*.
interpret = *conjecture*.
investigate, ἐρευνάω, ἐξετάζω.
invisible, ἀφανής.
invite, καλέω.
iron, σίδηρος.
island, νῆσος (ἡ).
issue, (verb) = *go out, the issue* (of events), τὰ ἀποβαίνοντα or ἐκβαίνοντα, also in singular.
Italy, Ἰταλία.

J.

jar, πίθος, ἀμφορεύς.
javelin, παλτόν, ἀκόντιον.
jealousy, φθόνος: *under jealousy*, ἐπίφθονος (dat.).
join, (trans.) ζεύγνυμι, συνάπτω, (intrans.) προσχωρέω: *join forces*, συνίσταμαι, συμμίγνυμι.
journey, ὁδός (ἡ), πορεία.
joy, χαρά.
joyful, joyfully = *glad, gladly*.
judge, κριτής, δικαστής.
judgment, (1) κρίσις (ἡ); (2) γνώμη.
jump down, καταπηδάω.
Juno, Ἡρα.
Jupiter, Ζεύς.
just, δίκαιος: *just now*, ἄρτι, ἀρτίως.
justice, δίκη, δικαιοσύνη.
justly, δικαίως.

K.

keep, ἔχω, or = *remain, continue*; *keep* (doing, &c.), often rendered by the imperfect.
kid, ἔριφος.
kill, ἀποκτείνω: *am killed*, usually ἀποθνήσκω.
kind, γένος (τύ), εἶδος (τό): *kind of*, often rendered by τις: *this kind of, what kind*, &c. See sort.
kindness, εὐεργεσία (often in pl.): *do a kindness*, εὐεργετέω, εὖ ποιέω (acc.), χαρίζομαι (dat.).
king, βασιλεύς: *like a king*, βασιλικῶς.
kingdom, βασιλεία, ἀρχή.
kinsman, συγγενής.
knee, γόνυ (τό).
know, γιγνώσκω, οἶδα, ἐπίσταμαι.
knowledge, ἐπιστήμη: *without the knowledge of*, see secretly.
known, γνωστός: (of persons) γνώριμος.

L.

labour, πόνος ; (verb) πονέω.
Lacedaemonian, Λακεδαιμόνιος.
Laconia, ἡ Λακωνική.
ladder, κλῖμαξ (-ακος), ἡ.
lake, λίμνη.
lamb, ἀμνός.
lame, χωλός.
Lampsacus, man of, Λαμψακηνός.
land, γῆ, χώρα.
last, ὕστατος, τελευταῖος : *at last,* τέλος.
last, (verb) = *endure, remain.*
late, (adv.) ὀψέ.
lately, ἄρτι, ἀρτίως.
laugh, γελάω : *laugh at,* ἐγγελάω, σκώπτω.
launch, καθέλκω, ἀνάγω (ναῦς).
law, νόμος.
lawless, ἄνομος.
lazy = *idle.*
lead, ἄγω, ἡγέομαι, also = *induce* ; (of a road) φέρω : *lead back,* κατάγω : *lead a life,* ἄγω βίον, βιοτεύω.
leader, ἡγεμών.
leap into, εἰσπηδάω : *leap upon,* ἐπιπηδάω.
learn, μανθάνω, = *hear,* πυνθάνομαι, ἀκούω.
learning, μάθησις (ἡ), or τὸ μαθεῖν.
least, ἐλάχιστος : *at least,* γε : *not in the least,* οὐδαμῶς.
leave, λείπω : *leave behind,* παραλείπω, ἀπολείπω : *leave* (a place) = *depart from.*
left (hand), ἀριστερὰ (χείρ) : *left wing* (of an army) εὐώνυμον (κέρας).
leg, σκέλος (τό), κνήμη.
leisure, σχολή : *have leisure,* σχολάζω.
lend, χράω (in 1 aor. only); (of money) δανείζω.
length, μῆκος (τό) : *at length* = *at last,* also δή.

less, ἥσσων, ἐλάσσων, (adv.) ἧσσον, ἔλασσον : *much less,* μὴ ὅτι (after οὐδέ).
let (= *allow, let go*), ἀφίημι.
letter, ἐπιστολή.
libations, pour, σπένδω.
liberty, ἐλευθερία.
lie, *lie down* (κατά)κειμαι : *lie below,* ὑπόκειμαι : *lie beside,* παράκειμαι.
life, βίος.
lift up, (ἀν)αίρω, ἀνορθόω.
light, (noun) φῶς (τό) : (verb) ἅπτω, καίω.
like, (adj.) ὅμοιος : *a man like* (you, &c.), οἷος (σύ, &c.).
like, (verb) = *wish* or *love* ; *I should like* (to do), often ἡδέως ἄν (with opt.).
likely (is), εἰκός (ἐστί), ἔοικε : *likely* (to do), οἷος, (with infin. .
likewise, ὁμοίως, ὡσαύτως : (= *besides*) προσέτι.
Lilliput, use Μικράπολις.
Lilliputian, Μικραπολίτης.
line (of battle), τάξις (ἡ).
lion, λέων (-οντος).
listen to = *hear, obey.*
little, μικρός : *a little,* μιρκόν τι (with partitive gen.).
live, (1) ζάω. (2) βίον (δι)άγω : *live in* = *dwell in* ; *live on,* τρέφομαι ἀπό, ζάω ἀπό.
load = *burden.*
loaded, μεστός (gen.).
loaf, ἄρτος.
log, ξύλον.
long, μακρός, (both of place and time) ; *long ago,* πάλαι : *as long as,* ὅσον χρόνον, ἕως.
look, βλέπω, σκοπέω, ὁράω : *look after,* ἐπιμελέομαι (gen.) ; *look at,* προσβλέπω : *look for,* ζητέω, ἐρευνάω : *look up,* ἀναβλέπω.
lord, δεσπότης.
lose, ἀπόλλυμι, στερέομαι (gen.) ; *lose* (one's) way, ἀποπλανάομαι.
loss, am at a, ἀπορέω.

loud, μέγας, (adv.) μέγα or μεγάλῃ (τῇ) φωνῇ.

luxury, τρυφή: *in luxury*, τρυφῇ, τρυφερῶς.

Lycurgus, Λυκοῦργος.

M.

mad, am, μαίνομαι.

magistrate, ἄρχων.

magnificently, μεγαλοπρεπῶς.

mainland, ἤπειρος (ἡ).

main body, στρατιά.

make, ποιέω (often in middle).

make for = *go* or *sail towards*.

man, ἄνθρωπος, (opp. to woman) ἀνήρ: *a man* (indefinite) τις.

man-of-war, τριήρης (ἡ).

manage (affairs), πράσσω : *manage* (men), μεταχειρίζω or = *rule*.

many, πολλοί.

march, πορεύομαι, (of a general invading) ἐλαύνω: *march abreast*, ἐπιπάρειμι.

market place, ἀγορά.

marry (a wife), γαμέω, ἄγομαι.

massive, στερεός (στερρός).

master (of a house), δεσπότης, (in a school) διδάσκαλος : (= *trainer*) ἐπιστάτης : *am master*, κρατέω.

matter, πρᾶγμα, (often omitted) ; *it matters* (much, &c.), (πολύ, &c.) διαφέρει: *what is the matter?* τί ἐστι ; or τί πάσχει (τις) ;

may (do, &c.), ἔξεστι.

mean (to do), θέλω, (to say) λέγω.

means, by no, οὐδαμῶς.

meanwhile, ἐν τούτῳ.

measures, take, = *consult* (intrans.)

meat, κρέας (τό), in plural.

meet, ἐπιτυγχάνω, ἐντυγχάνω, ἀπαντάω (dat.), (in battle) συμμίγνυμι, συμβάλλω, ἀνθίσταμαι, also = *come together*.

meeting, σύλλογος, σύνοδος.

Megarian, Μεγαρεύς.

merely, = *only*, also οὐδὲν ἄλλο ἤ.

messenger, ἄγγελος.

methinks, δοκεῖ μοι, οἶμαι.

middle, midst, μέσος: *in the middle of*, ἐν μέσῳ, or μεταξύ with participle.

might, (noun) = *power*; (verb) see may; *when one might* (do, &c.), ἐξόν (μοι, &c.).

mile, = *eight stades*.

milk, γάλα (τό).

Milo, Μίλων (-ωνος).

mind, φρήν (ἡ): *have in mind*, ἐν νῷ ἔχω, ἐννοέω.

mind one's business, τὰ ἑαυτοῦ πράσσειν.

miserable, ἄθλιος.

miserably, ἀθλίως, κακῶς.

misery, κακοπάθεια.

misfortune, συμφορά, δυστυχία.

miss, ἁμαρτάνω, ἀποτυγχάνω (gen.).

mistake, ἁμαρτάνω.

modest, μέτριος, σώφρων.

money, ἀργύριον.

month, μήν (ὁ).

moon, σελήνη.

moor (ships), ὁρμίζω. See also anchor.

more, (adj.) πλείων ; (adv.) πλέον, μᾶλλον.

morning, ἕως (-ους), ἡ; *in the morning*. πρωί, (πρῶ).

morrow, αὔριον, ἡ ὑστεραία.

mortal, θνητός.

mother, μήτηρ.

motionless, ἀκίνητος.

mount (a horse), ἀναβαίνω (ἐπί), (a hill) ἐπιβαίνω (ἐπί).

mountain, ὄρος (τό).

mouse, μῦς.

mouth, στόμα (τό) : (of a river) ἐκβολή.

move, (trans.) κινέω, (intrans.) κινέομαι: *move* (from a place) μεθίσταμαι, or = *depart*: *move on*, = *advance* ; *move round* (of the earth, &c.), στρέφεσθαι περί.

much, πολύs: as *much* as, ὅσον: *too much*, ἄγαν, λίαν: *much less*, see less.
mud, πηλός.
muddy, θολερός.
multitude, πλῆθος (τό), ὅμιλος.
murder, (noun) φόνος: (verb), φονεύω, ἀποκτείνω.
must (do, &c.), δεῖ, or use the verbal adj. in -τέον.
muster (forces), συλλέγω.

N.

name, (noun) ὄνομα (τό): (verb) ὀνομάζω, καλέω.
Naples, Νεάπολις (ἡ).
narrow, στενός.
nasty, ῥυπαρός.
native, ἐγχώριος, πατρῷος.
nature, φύσις (ἡ).
navy, ναυτικόν.
near, ἐγγύς, πλησίον (gen.).
nearly, σχεδόν, μόνον οὐ, or use ὀλίγου δεῖν with infin.
necessity, ἀνάγκη.
neck, τράχηλος.
need, there is, δεῖ.
neglect (verb), ἀμελέω.
neighbour, ὁ πλησίον (usually plural).
neither . . . nor, οὔτε . . . οὔτε (μήτε . . . μήτε).
nest, νεοσσιά.
never, οὔποτε (μήποτε).
news, τὰ ἀγγελλόμενα, also καινόν: *bring news*, (κατ)αγγέλλω.
next (of place), ἐγγύτατα, ἐγγυτάτω, also ἐχόμενος: (of time) μετὰ ταῦτα, ἐντεῦθεν: *next day*, τῇ ὑστεραίᾳ.
night, νύξ (ἡ): *by night*, νυκτός.
nightingale, ἀηδών (ἡ).
nobleman, εὐγενής: *nobles*, οἱ ἄριστοι.
nobody, no one, οὐδείς (μηδείς).
noise, θόρυβος, ψόφος.

noon, μεσημβρία, μέση ἡμέρα, μέσον ἡμέρας.
not, οὐ, οὐκ, οὐχ before aspirates, (μή): *not at all*, οὐδαμῶς: *not even*, οὐδέ (μηδέ): *not only*, οὐχ ὅτι: *not only not*, οὐχ ὅπως: *not yet*, οὔπω (μήπω): *not* . . . *nor*, οὐ . . . οὐδέ (μή . . . μηδέ): *and not*, οὐδέ . . . μηδέ: *no longer*, οὐκέτι (μηκέτι).
nothing, οὐδέν (μηδέν).
now, νῦν, ἤδη: (in continuing a story) δέ.
nowhere, οὐδαμοῦ.
number, ἀριθμός: *a number of* = *many.*

O.

oak, δρῦς (ἡ).
oath, ὅρκος: *on oath* = *having sworn.*
obey, πείθομαι (dat.).
oblige, χαρίζομαι (dat.).
obol, ὀβολός.
observe, (1) = *see.* (2) = *say.*
obstinately (of defence), κρατερῶς, or use διακαρτερεῖν with part.
obtain, τυγχάνω (gen.), κτάομαι, also λαμβάνω.
occur. See under happen.
offer, δίδωμι: *offer sacrifice*, θύω.
officer (in army), λοχαγός; (=*attendant*) ὑπηρετής.
oil, ἔλαιον.
old (in time), παλαιός, ἀρχαῖος: *old man*, γέρων:—*years old*, —ἔτη γεγονώς.
omen, οἰωνός.
once, (=*formerly*) ποτέ: (=*one time*) ἅπαξ: *at once* = *directly.*
only, μόνον: *not only.* See not.
open, (verb) ἀνοίγω, (adj.) use part. of verb.
opinion, γνώμη, δόξα: *give opinion*, γνώμην ἀποφαίνομαι.
opponent, ἐναντίος.
oppose, ἀνθίσταμαι (dat.).

opposite, ἀντίος, ἐναντίος.
oracle, χρησμός.
orator, ῥήτωρ (-ορος).
order, (noun) τάξις (ἡ): give orders, κελεύω, ἐπιστέλλω: in order that, ἵνα, ὅπως.
orderly, εὔτακτος, κόσμιος, (adv.) εὐτάκτως, ἐν τάξει: without order, ἄτακτος.
other, ἄλλος, (of two) ἕτερος.
ought, χρή, δεῖ, or use verbal adj. in -τέον.
outside, outer, ἔξω.
overpower, κρατέω (gen.).
overtake, καταλαμβάνω.
owe, ὀφείλω.
own (one's), ἑαυτοῦ.
ox, βοῦς.

P.

pace, (verb) = walk about.
pain, ἄλγος (τό): have pain, ἀλγέω.
pains, take, πονέω, σπουδάζω.
palace, βασίλειον (also in plural).
palisade, σταύρωμα (τό).
parent, γονεύς.
park, παράδεισος.
part, μέρος (τό).
pass, (noun) ἐσβολή.
pass by, παρέρχομαι: pass through, διέρχομαι: pass (time), διάγω.
path, ἀτραπός (ἡ), ὁδός (ἡ).
pay, (noun) μισθός: (verb) ἀποδίδωμι: pay (tribute), ἀποφέρω.
peace, εἰρήνη.
pelt, βάλλω.
people, λεώς (in Homer λαός in pl.), δῆμος: (of a town) οἱ πολῖται.
perceive, αἰσθάνομαι (gen.), ὁράω.
perched (on) = sitting (on).
perform, πράσσω, ποιέω, (ἐκ)-τελέω.
perhaps, ἴσως.
perish, ἀπόλλυμαι, θνήσκω.
persecute, διώκω.

Persian, Πέρσης, (with fem. nouns) Περσίς (-ίδος).
persist = continue (doing).
persuade, πείθω (acc.).
pestilential, λοιμώδης.
Philip, Φίλιππος.
philosopher, φιλόσοφος.
philosophy, φιλοσοφία.
Phoenician, Φοῖνιξ.
physician, ἰατρός.
picked (men), ἐπίλεκτοί.
pigeon, περιστερά.
pin, περόνη, κερκίς (-ίδος), ἡ.
pine-tree, πίτυς (-υος), ἡ.
pity, (noun) οἶκτος, ἔλεος: (verb) οἰκτίζω.
place, (noun) τόπος, χωρίον: to a place where or whence = thither, where or whence.
place, (verb) τίθημι, ἵστημι, καθίστημι: take place, γίγνομαι.
plain, (noun) πεδίον: (adj.) = evident.
plainly = evidently.
plank, δοκός (ἡ).
Plato, Πλάτων.
pleasant, ἡδύς.
pleasantly, ἡδέως.
please, ἀρέσκω, χαρίζομαι (dat.); am pleased, ἥδομαι: it pleases (me), δοκεῖ (μοι).
plentiful, plenty of, πολύς, ἄφθονος.
plot, (noun) ἐπιβουλή: (verb) ἐπιβουλεύω, (dat.).
plough, (verb) ἀρόω: (noun) ἄροτρον.
plunder, (verb) ἁρπάζω, ληΐζομαι: (noun) = spoil.
poet, ποιητής.
poison, φάρμακον.
pollute, μιαίνω.
poor, πένης.
position, am in a, διακεῖμαι (with adv.).
possess, ἔχω: get possession, κτάομαι, κατέχω.
possessions, κτήματα.

possible, δυνατόν : *it is possible,* also ἔξεστι.

post (military), τάξις (ἡ).

postern gate, πυλίς (-ίδος), ἡ.

potter, κεραμεύς.

poverty, πενία.

power, δύναμις (ἡ) : *it is in* (one's) *power,* ἔξεστι.

practise, ἀσκέω, μελετάω.

praise, (noun) ἔπαινος : (verb) ἐπαινέω.

pray (to gods), εὔχομαι. See also ask.

prefer, προαιρέομαι.

prepare, (trans.) παρασκευάζω : (intrans.) παρασκευάζομαι. The middle is also commonly used for the active voice.

present, am, πάρειμι : *present* (circumstances), τὰ παρόντα : *men of present day,* οἱ νῦν, &c.

present, (noun) δῶρον.

presently = *soon, directly.*

press on, ἐπείγομαι, or σπεύδων with verb of motion.

pretend, προσποιέομαι.

prevent = *hinder.*

priest, ἱερεύς.

prince = *king.*

prison, δεσμωτήριον.

prisoner = *captive.*

prize, τιμή : (in games, &c.) ἆθλον.

proceed = *advance; proceed* (to do), usually rendered by imperf.

proclaim, κηρύσσω, ἀνειπεῖν : *without proclamation,* ἀκήρυκτος.

procure, = *obtain.*

profitable, ὠφέλιμος, σύμφορος.

promise, (verb) ὑπισχνέομαι : (noun) πίστις, ὑπόσχεσις (ἡ).

proof, τεκμήριον.

proper, it is, πρέπει, προσήκει.

property, χρήματα.

propitious, = *favourable.*

proportion, = *part; in proportion,* ἀνὰ or κατὰ λόγον.

propose, = *intend, wish.*

prosecute, διώκω.

prosper, εὐτυχέω.

prosperity, εὐτυχία.

prosperous, εὐτυχής.

protect = *defend.*

provide, παρέχω, παρασκευάζω.

province, ἀρχή.

provisions, ἐπιτήδεια, σιτία.

provoke, = *make angry,* ὀργίζω.

prudent, σώφρων.

public, δημόσιος : *public property,* τὰ δημόσια.

pull up (a horse), ἐφίστημι (in transitive tenses).

pulpit, βῆμα (τό), perhaps λογεῖον.

punish, κολάζω, τιμωρέομαι.

purple (robe), πορφυρίς (-ίδος), ἡ.

purpose, βούλη, also γνώμη.

purse, βαλάντιον.

pursue, διώκω.

put, τίθημι : *put forth* (branches, &c.), φύω : *put on* (clothes), ἐνδύω.

put out, προτείνω, ἐξείρω : *put out* (fires), κατασβέννυμι.

Q.

quantity of = *much.*

quarrel, στασιάζω.

queen, βασίλεια.

quick, ταχύς.

quickly, ταχέως, or use φθάσας.

quiet, ἥσυχος, (of disposition) ἀπράγμων.

quit oneself = *behave.*

quite, πάνυ, σφόδρα, μάλα.

R.

rain, ὄμβρος, ὑετός.

raise, αἴρω : *raise again,* ἐπανορθόω.

rank (military), τάξις (ἡ).

rash, θρασύς, τολμηρός.

rashly, θρασέως, ἀπερισκέπτως.

rashness, θρασύτης (-ητος), ἡ.

rather, μᾶλλον.

ravage, τέμνω.

reach = *come to,* ἐφικνέομαι.

reach, a certain point, ἀνήκω.
read, ἀναγιγνώσκω.
ready, ἕτοιμος : *get ready*, παρασκευάζομαι.
really, τῷ ὄντι, ἀληθῶς.
reaper, θεριστής (-οῦ).
rear (of army), οἱ ὄπισθεν.
reason, (1) = *cause*. (2) λόγος (the faculty).
rebuild, ἀνοικοδομέω, ἐπανίστημι.
receive, λαμβάνω : (= *welcome*) δέχομαι.
recognise, (ἀνα)γνωρίζω.
recover, ἀναλαμβάνω : (from a disease) ἰσχύω, also ἀναλαμβάνω (ἐμαυτόν).
red, ἐρυθρός.
refuse, οὐκ ἐθέλω, οὔ φημι (with fut. infin.).
reign, (verb) βασιλεύω, ἄρχω.
rejoice, χαίρω.
relate (story), διηγέομαι.
relation, συγγενής.
relieve = *succour*.
remain, μένω, καταμένω, διαμένω.
remember, μέμνημαι, μνημονεύω.
removable, ἐξαιρετός.
rend asunder, διαρρήγνυμι.
repair, (verb) ἐπισκευάζω : (noun) ἐπισκευή.
repel, ἀπωθέω (often in middle).
repent, μεταμέλει (μοι).
report, ἀπαγγέλλω.
reprove, μέμφομαι, ἐπιτιμάω (dat.).
repute, δόξα, τιμή : *am reputed*, δοκέω.
request, ἀξιόω, αἰτέω, also = *bid*.
rescue, come to the, (ἐπι)βοηθέω (dat.).
resentment (of the gods), φθόνος.
resist = *oppose*.
resolved, it is, δοκεῖ.
respect, (verb) = *honour*.
rest, ἀναπαύομαι : rest on. See support (2).
rest, the, οἱ λοιποί, ἕτεροι.
restore, ἀποδίδωμι, ἀποφέρω.

restrain, κατέχω.
retire, retreat, ἀναχωρέω. See also depart.
return (trans.) = *restore*, (intrans.) κατέρχομαι, πάλιν ἥκω : *return home*, ἀπονοστέω : *in return*, αὖ, or use compound with ἀντί.
reveal, ἐκφαίνω, ἐξηγέομαι.
review (of troops), ἐξέτασις (ἡ) ; (verb) ἐξετάζω.
reward, δῶρον, τίμη : *am rewarded*, ἀντιλαμβάνω.
rhinoceros, ῥινόκερως (-ωτος).
rich, πλούσιος.
riches, πλοῦτος.
ride, ἱππεύω : *ride away*, ἀπελαύνω : *ride forward*, *ride on*, προϊππεύω, προελαύνω: *ride up*, προσελαύνω.
right, ὀρθός, δίκαιος : *have a right*, δίκαιός εἰμι, or ἔξεστί (μοι).
right (hand) on the, δεξιός.
rightly, ὀρθῶς.
ring, δακτύλιος.
rise, ἀνίσταμαι, and the intrans. tenses of the active voice ; (of the sun) ἀνατέλλω.
risk, run, κινδυνεύω.
river, ποταμός.
road, ὁδός (ἡ).
rob, ἀφαιρέω, ἀποστερέω.
robber, λῃστής, κλέπτης.
rock, πέτρα.
Roman, Ῥωμαῖος.
roof, ὀροφή.
rope, σπάρτον, σχοινίον.
rose, ῥόδον.
rout, (noun) φυγή, τροπή : (verb) εἰς φυγὴν τρέπω or καθίστημι.
row, ἐλαύνω.
rule, ἄρχω (gen.).
ruler, ἄρχων, ἡγεμών (-όνος).
run, τρέχω : *run away*, ἀποδιδράσκω : *run past*, παρατρέχω : *run up*, προστρέχω, or δρόμῳ προσέρχομαι.
rush, φέρομαι, (with or without δρόμῳ) : *rush in*, εἰσπίπτω.

S.

sacrifice (verb), θύω (often in middle).

sacrifices, ἱερά.

safe, ἀσφαλής.

safety, ἀσφάλεια, σωτηρία: *in safety,* ἀσφαλῶς, ἐν ἀσφαλεῖ.

sail, πλέω: *sail across,* διαπλέω: *sail along,* παραπλέω: *sail away,* ἀποπλέω.

sailor, ναύτης.

sake of, for the, ἕνεκα.

same, the, ὁ αὐτός (αὐτός).

Samian, Σάμιος.

Sardis, Σάρδεις (αἱ).

satrap, σατράπης.

save, (verb) σώζω.

save (= *except*), εἰ μή.

say, φημί, λέγω.

saying, λόγος.

scatter, διασπείρω, σκεδάννυμι.

scout, σκοπός.

scream (verb), use ὀλολυγῇ χρῆσθαι.

Scythian, Σκύθης.

sea, θάλασσα.

season, ὥρα, (= *fitting time*) καιρός.

seat, ἕδρα: *seat oneself* = *sit.*

second, δεύτερος, ἕτερος: *a second time,* (τὰ) δεύτερα, αὖθις.

secretly, λάθρα, or use λανθάνω.

see, ὁράω.

seek, ζητέω. See also look for.

seem, δοκέω, φαίνομαι: also use ὁρᾶσθαι.

seize = *take,* also ἁρπάζω.

sell, πωλέω, ἀποδίδομαι.

send, πέμπω: *send for,* μεταπέμπομαι: *send a message, send word,* (ἀπ)αγγέλλω: *send forward,* προπέμπω.

sentinel = *guard.*

serve, δουλεύω, θητεύω, (in the army) στρατεύω.

servant, δοῦλος, also παῖς.

service (= *kindness*), εὐεργεσία: *do a service,* ὑπουργέω, ὑπηρετέω (dat.).

set, = *place*; *set up,* ἀνίστημι: *set out,* (ἐξ)ὁρμάομαι: *set on fire,* καίω.

settle, (intrans.) ἱδρύομαι, (κατ)οικίζομαι.

severe, χαλεπός.

shade, σκιά.

share, μέρος (τό).

sharp, ὀξύς.

sheep, οἶς, (in plural) πρόβατα.

shelter, καταφυγή.

shepherd, ποιμήν (-ένος).

ship, ναῦς: *ship of war,* τριήρης (ἡ).

shoot, τοξεύω, βάλλω.

shore, αἰγιαλός, or use γῆ.

short, βραχύς.

should, (= *ought*), δεῖ, χρή, or use verbal adj.

shoulder, ὦμος.

shout, (noun) βοή, (verb) βοάω: (in battle), ἀλαλάζω.

show, δείκνυμι, φαίνω.

shut, (κατα)κλείω.

Sicily, Σικελία.

side, (of man or animal) πλευρά and πλευρόν: *on the side of* (= *party*), πρός (gen.); *on the other side,* πέραν (gen.).

sight, ὄψις (ἡ).

sign, signal, σημεῖον: *give the signal,* σημαίνω: *make a sign* (to anyone), νεύω.

silence, σιγή.

silent, am, σιγάω, σιωπάω.

silver, ἄργυρος.

simpleton, μῶρος, ἀνόητος.

simplicity, εὐήθεια.

since, (causal) ἐπεί, ὡς: (temporal) ἐπεί, also ἐξ οὗ.

sing, ᾄδω.

single, = *one*; *not a single* (one), οὐδὲ εἷς.

sister, ἀδελφή.

sit, sit down, κάθημαι, καθέζομαι: *sit* (at meals), κατάκειμαι, *sit by* or *beside,* παρακάθημαι; *sit round,* περικάθημαι.

size, μέγεθος (τό).

skilled, ἔμπειρος.

sky, οὐρανός.

slaughter, φόνος, σφαγή.

slave, δοῦλος.

sleep, (verb) καθεύδω, κοιμάομαι: (noun) ὕπνος.

slowly, βραδέως, (of motion) βάδην.

smile, μειδιάω, γελάω.

snatch up, ἀναρπάζω.

so (= thus), οὕτω(s) : (in narrative) οὖν, τοίνυν : so that, so as to, ὥστε : so great, τοσοῦτος : so much, τόσον, τοσοῦτον.

soldier, στρατιώτης.

some, some one, τις, (in pl. also), ἔνιοι, (ἔστιν οἵ) : some ... others, οἱ μέν ... οἱ δέ or ἄλλοι ... ἄλλοι.

sometimes, ἐνίοτε.

son, υἱός, παῖς ; the son of—, often ὁ τοῦ —.

soon, τάχα : as soon as, ἐπεί, ἐπειδή, (ἐπειδάν with subj.) followed by τάχιστα : be too soon, φθάνειν.

sooner, (1) of time, πρότερον. (2) = rather.

soothsayer, μάντις.

sorrow = grief.

sort, this, τοῖος, τοιοῦτος : of what sort, οἷος : every sort, παντοῖος.

source (of a river), πηγή (often in pl.).

sovereign = king, ruler, also τύραννος.

sovereignty, ἀρχή.

sow, (κατα)σπείρω.

Spaniard, Ἴβηρος.

spare, φείδομαι (gen.).

sparingly, φειδωλῶς.

speak, λέγω, φθέγγομαι.

spear, δόρυ (τό), λόγχη.

speed, τάχος (τό) : at full speed, ἀνὰ κράτος.

spend (money), ἀναλίσκω: (time), διατρίβω.

spirit, θυμός. See also courage.

spoil, λεία.

spot = place.

spread = scatter.

spring, ἔαρ (τό), (of water) κρήνη : spring up, ἐκφύομαι and intrans. tenses of active voice.

square, τετράγωνος.

stade, στάδιον (pl. usually στάδιοι).

stand, ἵσταμαι, and intrans. tenses of active voice ; stand on, ἐφίσταμαι : stand together, συνίσταμαι.

start = set out.

state, πόλις : (of affairs), πράγματα.

station, (verb) = place.

stay. μένω, also διατρίβω.

steal, κλέπτω, συλάω.

steep, προσάντης.

step, (noun) βῆμα (τό) : (verb) βαίνω, βαδίζω.

stick, ῥάβδος (ἡ).

still, (adj.) = quiet ; (adv.) ἔτι.

stone, λίθος : of stone, λίθινος : stone to death, καταπετρόω.

stop, (trans.) παύω, (intrans.) παύομαι.

storm, χειμών (ὁ) : (take) by storm, κατὰ κράτος.

story, λόγος, μῦθος.

straight, εὐθύς, ὀρθός : (adv.) εὐθύ.

straightway = directly.

strange, δεινός, θαυμαστός.

stranger, ξένος.

stream, ῥόος, ποταμός.

street, ὁδός (ἡ).

stretch, (ἀνα)τείνω.

strike, παίω, πατάσσω : (in passive) πλήσσω : (with a missile) βάλλω.

strip, ἐκδύω.

strive, διατείνομαι, πειράομαι : strive after, ἐπιτείνομαι (εἰς), σπεύδω.

strong, ἰσχυρός.

subject (= matter), πρᾶγμα : subjects (of a king), ἀρχόμενοι, ὑπήκοοι : make subject, δουλόω, ὑποτίθημι.

submit, (=*yield*), ἐνδίδωμι, ὑφίεμαι : *submit to*, (=*endure*).

succeed, (1) εὐτυχέω. (2) =*follow*, ἐπιγίγνομαι : *succeed in*, κατορθόω (acc.).

succour, βοηθέω (dat.).

such, τοιοῦτος, (τοῖος), τοιόσδε.

suddenly, ἐξαίφνης.

suffer, (1) πάσχω. (2) = *endure*.

sufficient, (adj.) ἱκανός : (adv.) ἅλις.

sum (of money), ἀργύριον, or use χρήματα.

summer, θέρος (τό).

sun, ἥλιος : *sunrise* (*at*), ἅμα ἡλίῳ ἀνατέλλοντι : *sunset*, ἡλίου δυσμαί.

sup, δειπνέω.

superior, κρείσσων, ἀμείνων : *am superior*, περίειμι, διαφέρω (gen.).

supper, δεῖπνον.

support, (verb) τρέφω : (noun) τροφή : (=*prop*) ἐρείδω.

suppose, οἴομαι, (οἶμαι in conversations).

sure, (1) =*certain*. (2) πιστός : *am sure* (of) = *am certain*.

surely = *certainly* ; *surely not*, οὐ δῆτα, οὐ δήπου.

surprise, (1) ἐκπλήσσω. (2) = *take unawares*, use λαθών or ἀπροσδόκητον λαβεῖν : *am surprised*, θαυμάζω, ἐκπλήσσομαι.

surrender, (trans. and intrans.) ἐνδίδωμι, (intrans. only) ὑφίεμαι.

surround, κυκλόομαι : (with a wall) περιβάλλω (act. and mid.).

survey, ἐφοράω, σκοπέω, θεάομαι.

survive, περιγίγνομαι.

suspect, ὑποπτεύω.

sustain, (an attack) δέχομαι.

swallow, χελιδών (ἡ).

swear, ὄμνυμι.

sweet, ἡδύς.

sweetly (of singing, &c.), λιγυρῶς.

swim, νέω : *swim up to*, προσνέω.

sword, ξίφος (τό).

Syracuse, Συράκουσαι (αἱ).

T.

table, τράπεζα.

take, λαμβάνω, αἱρέω : *take away*, ἀφαιρέω (mostly in mid.) ; *take back*, ἀπολαμβάνω : *take charge of*, ἐπιμελέομαι (gen.) ; *take off* (clothes), ἀποδύω : *take pains*, πονέω, σπουδάζω : *take prisoner* = *capture*; *take up*, ἀναλαμβάνω: *take up arms*, ὅπλα ἀνταίρομαι, or = *make war*; *take place*, see place.

talent, τάλαντον.

talk, λαλέω, διαλέγω.

tall, (of persons) μακρός, (of things) ὑψηλός.

task = *work*.

teach, διδάσκω.

teacher, διδάσκαλος.

Tegean, Τεγεάτης.

tell, (1) εἰπεῖν. (2) =*bid* ; *I cannot tell*, οὐκ οἶδα.

temperate, σώφρων.

temple, ἱερόν.

tend, (flocks or herds). See feed.

tent, σκηνή.

terrible, δεινός.

territory, γῆ, χώρα.

than, ἤ, or by *gen.* after comparative.

thank = *am grateful*.

that, (in statements of fact) ὅτι : (of purpose), ἵνα, ὅπως.

Theban, Θηβαῖος.

Thebes, Θῆβαι.

theft, κλοπή.

then, (1) of time, τότε, ἐνταῦθα : (= *afterwards*) ἔπειτα. (2) = *therefore*.

there, ἐκεῖ, (= *thither*) ἐκεῖσε : *am there*, πάρειμι.

therefore, οὖν, τοίνυν.

thereupon, ἐνταῦθα, ἐκ τούτου.

thick, παχύς.

thief, κλέπτης.

think, οἴομαι, νομίζω, also δοκεῖ (μοι) : *am thought* (to be, &c.), δοκέω.

thirsty, am, διψάω.
thither, ἐκεῖσε.
though = although; as though, ὡς, ὥσπερ.
thoughtless = foolish.
Thrace, Θρᾴκη.
Thracian, Θρᾷξ.
threaten, ἀπειλέω (dat.).
thrice, τρίς.
throne, use ἀρχή.
throw, βάλλω, ῥίπτω: throw away, ἀποβάλλω: throw over, ὑπερβάλλω.
Thurian (land), Θουριὰς (γῆ).
thus, οὕτω(s), ὧδε.
Tigris, Τίγρης (ποταμός).
tile, κέραμος.
time, χρόνος: at the same time, ἅμα: by this time, ἤδη: in our time, ἐφ᾽ ἡμῶν.
tired, am, κάμνω, also ἀπειπεῖν.
to and fro, (walk), περιπατέω.
to-day, σήμερον.
to-morrow, αὔριον.
together, ὁμοῦ, ἅμα, or use compound with σύν.
tomb, τάφος.
tongue, γλῶσσα.
too (1) = also. (2) λίαν, ἄγαν, also rendered by comparative.
tooth, ὀδούς (ὁ).
top (of), ἄκρος (adj.), ἄκρα (noun).
toss (about), διαρρίπτω.
touch, θιγγάνω, ἐφάπτομαι: touch at, (προσ)ίσχω ἐπί or εἰς.
tower, πύργος.
town-hall, πρυτανεῖον.
trainer, ἐπιστάτης.
traitor, προδότης.
trap, πάγη.
treacherous, ἄπιστος.
treachery, ἀπιστία, προδοσία.
treasure, (noun) θησαυρός, (verb) θησαυρίζω.
treat, χράομαι: am treated, πάσχω (with adv.).
treaty, σπονδή (in plural).
tree, δένδρον.

tribute, φόρος: pay tribute, ὑποτελέω, ἀποφέρω.
trifling = small.
trouble, πόνος: give trouble, ὄχλον or πράγματα παρέχω.
troublesome, ἐπαχθής, λυπηρός.
truce = treaty.
true, ἀληθής, ἀληθινός.
truly = really.
truth, ἀλήθεια: the truth, τὸ ἀληθές, τὸ σαφές: speak truth, ἀληθεύω.
trust, πιστεύω.
trustworthy, πιστός.
try, πειράομαι.
turn, τρέπω, στρέφω: turn out = become: am turned into, γίγνομαι.
twice, δίς.
tyrant, τύραννος.

U.

unable, ἀδύνατος: am unable = cannot.
unacquainted, ἄπειρος (gen.).
unawares, λάθρα, or use λανθάνω.
uncertain, ἄδηλος: am uncertain, ἀπορέω, οὐκ οἶδα.
uncover, ἐκκαλύπτω.
understand, ἐπίσταμαι.
undertake, ὑποδέχομαι, ἐπιχειρέω.
undeserved, ἀνάξιος, also παρὰ τὴν ἀξίαν.
undone, am, ὄλωλα.
unfair = unjust.
unfaithful, ἄπιστος.
unfortunate, δυστυχής: am unfortunate, δυστυχέω.
ungrateful, ἀχάριστος.
unhappy, ἄθλιος, δυστυχής.
unjust, ἄδικος: act unjustly, ἀδικέω.
unknown, ἀγνοούμενος, ἄγνωστος.
unless, εἰ (ἐὰν) μή.
unperceived. See unawares.
unpunished. See get off (punishment).
until, μέχρι, ἕως, πρίν.
unwisely = foolishly.

up, upwards, ἄνω.

use, (verb) χράομαι : (noun) *what is the use of?* τί ὠφελεῖ;

useless, ἄχρηστος, ἀχρεῖος.

utter (sounds), φθέγγομαι.

utterly (perish), πανωλέθρως.

V.

vainly, in vain, μάτην.

valiant, valiantly = *brave, bravely.*

valour = *courage.*

valuable, πολλοῦ ἄξιος, τίμιος : *more, less valuable,* πλείονος, μείονος ἄξιος.

value, τιμή.

vegetables, λάχανα.

vengeance, take = *avenge oneself.*

venture = *dare.*

very, μάλα, πάνυ, or use superlative.

vessel, (1) ἀγγεῖον. (2) = *ship.*

victims, σφάγια.

victory, νίκη.

vigorously, κατὰ κράτος.

village, κώμη.

villain, πονηρός.

violently, βίᾳ.

virtue, ἀρετή.

virtuous = *good.*

visible, φανερός : *am visible,* φαίνομαι.

vision, ὄψις (ἡ).

voice, φωνή.

void, κενός.

vote, ψῆφος (ἡ).

voyage, πλόος.

vulture, γύψ (-πος).

W.

wait, μένω : *wait about, wait for,* περιμένω.

walk, βαδίζω : *walk about,* περιπατέω.

wall, τοῖχος, (of a city) τεῖχος (τό).

want, (verb) δέομαι (gen.), or = *wish* : (noun) ἔνδεια, χρεία.

war, πόλεμος : *make war,* πολεμέω.

warn, νουθετέω, παραινέω (dat.).

wash = *bathe* ; *wash* (clothes) πλύνω.

waste (time), διατρίβω.

watch, φυλάσσω, τηρέω.

water, ὕδωρ (τό).

water-snake, ὕδρα.

way, ὁδός (ἡ) : *in* (one's) *way,* ἐμποδών : *give way* (see under give) ; *make* (one's) *way,* πορεύομαι, ἀφικνέομαι.

weak, ἀσθενής : *am weak,* ἀσθενέω.

wealthy = *rich,* also εὐδαίμων.

wear, ἔχω, φέρω.

weigh anchor, ἀνάγομαι, also (ναῦς) αἴρομαι.

weight, βάρος (τό).

well, (noun) φρέαρ (τό).

well, (adv.), εὖ, καλῶς : *am well* (in health), ὑγιαίνω : *it is well,* εὖ ἔχει.

what? τίς ; τί ; *what sort?* ποῖος ; (rel. and exclamatory) οἷος.

whatever, ὅτι (ὅστις).

when? πότε ; (rel.) ὅτε (ὅταν with subj.), ἐπεί.

whence? πόθεν ; (rel.) ὅθεν.

whenever, ὁπότε (ὁπόταν).

where? ποῦ ; (rel.) οὗ, ὅπου.

whereupon, ἐνταῦθα.

whether? πότερον ; (indirect) εἰ, εἴτε, *whether . . . or* εἴτε . . . εἴτε, (interrog.) πότερον . . . ἤ.

which, (rel.) ὅς ; *which* (of two)? πότερος ;

while, ἕως, ἐν ᾧ ; *while* (doing, &c.), use simple part. ; (with verb in indic. use δέ, with or without μέν in the previous clause ; *for a while,* χρόνον τινά, also τέως.

white, λευκός.

white (leprosy), λευκή (as a noun).

whither? ποῖ ; (rel.) οἷ, ὅποι.

who? τίς; (rel.) ὅς (ὅστις).
whoever, ὅστις.
whole, πᾶς with article, ὅλος.
why? τί; διὰ τί;
wide, width = broad, breadth.
wife, γυνή.
wild, ἄγριος: wild beast, θηρίον.
will, am willing = wish.
willing, (adj.) ἑκών, ἑκούσιος.
willingly, ἡδέως, προθύμως.
win, (a victory) νικάω, (a prize) κομίζομαι.
wind, ἄνεμος.
window, θυρίς (-ίδος), ἡ.
wine, οἶνος.
wing, πτέρυξ (-γος), ἡ, (of an army) κέρας (τό).
winter, χειμών (ὁ).
wisdom, σοφία, (τὸ) φρονεῖν.
wise, σόφος, φρόνιμος: am wise, σωφρονέω.
wish, βούλομαι, ἐθέλω (θέλω).
with, sometimes rendered by ἔχων.
within, (of place) = inside; (of time), use genitive.
without, ἄνευ, (of place) = outside.
wolf, λύκος.
woman, γυνή.
wonder, θαυμάζω.
wonderful, θαυμάσιος, θαυμαστός.
wood, (1) ξύλον. (2) = forest.
wooden, ξύλινος.

word, λόγος: in a word, τὸ σύμπαν.
work, (noun) ἔργον; (= labour) πόνος: (verb) ἐργάζομαι, πονέω.
world, γῆ, (= universe) κόσμος. who in the world? τίς ποτε;
worship, σέβομαι.
worth, worthy, ἄξιος: think or deem worthy, ἀξιόω: worth while, ἄξιον.
would that, εἴθε (with opt.), ὤφελον (with infin.).
wound, (verb) τιτρώσκω, τραυματίζω: (noun) τραῦμα (τό).
wretched = miserable.
write, γράφω.
wrong, do, ἀδικέω, ἁμαρτάνω.

Y.

yard, (measure); express by ὀργυιά, which = 2 yards, or by πλέθρον, = about 30 yards.
year, ἔτος (τό).
yellow, ξανθός.
yesterday, χθές, ἐχθές.
yet, (= nevertheless) ὅμως, (of time) ἔτι: not yet, οὔπω.
yield = submit.
yonder, ἐκεῖνος.
young, νέος: young bird, νεοσσός: young man, νεανίας, νεανίσκος.

THE END.

www.ingramcontent.com/pod-product-compliance
Lightning Source LLC
Chambersburg PA
CBHW022341020726
47500CB00004B/1223